THE PRESENT FUTURE

*He who holds the key to time
is the master of destiny*

By
Caroline Hunter

AuthorHouse™ UK Ltd.
500 Avebury Boulevard
Central Milton Keynes, MK9 2BE
www.authorhouse.co.uk
Phone: 08001974150

©2010 Caroline Hunter. All rights reserved.

No part of this book may be reproduced, stored in a retrieval system, or transmitted by any means without the written permission of the author.

First published by AuthorHouse 12/15/2010

ISBN: 978-1-4520-8233-2 (sc)

This book is printed on acid-free paper.

Acknowledgements

Special thanks to Vanessa and Jasmine for their invaluable help and my husband John for all his support.

CHAPTER ONE

PART ONE

DEVON, ENGLAND

THE TWENTY FIRST OF APRIL TWO THOUSAND AND NINETY ONE

Matt Jacobs was just ten years old when he first discovered he had the gift, a gift that would change his life in ways he never could have imagined.

Having lost his parents after they mysteriously disappeared at sea two years earlier, Matt was no stranger to life changing events. However, nothing could have prepared him for what was about to come.

It was a Friday afternoon, an exceptionally hot one for the time of year and Matt was on his way home from school, looking forward to the weekend. Most of all he was looking forward to having two days when he wouldn't have to endure the endless bullying of Rick Fowler. Rick Fowler was in the same year at school as Matt and for some reason, he had no idea why, Fowler seemed to hate him. Even in the heat of the afternoon sun, Matt felt himself shiver at the thought of Fowler, it seemed to him that Fowler was on a mission to make his life hell. He and his mates would gang up on Matt at every opportunity, making fun of him, and constantly making gibes about his parents. That was what upset him the most. They would taunt him by saying that his mum and dad had run out on him because they couldn't stand living with him any longer. Even though he knew this wasn't true, Matt was deeply hurt by it, he missed his parents very much and would often dream about them. However, for some reason, lately, their faces had started to become bleary, almost featureless and he was afraid that one day he would forget what they looked like altogether.

As he followed the usual route to the 'Old Forge' on the outskirts of Ottery St Mary, where he lived with his grandad, the sun pounded down scorching the earth beneath his feet. He walked along side the river Otter and was tempted to jump in and cool off. However he was halted by a sudden splash. A golden retriever had beaten him to it, chasing a stick which its owner had thrown. The dog scampered around, dipping its nose into the water trying to locate the stick. Then, having been successful, it emerged, stick in mouth, scrambling onto the bank, shaking itself off so close to Matt that he got an unexpected shower.

'Zandi' shouted the owner, 'come away from the poor lad'.

'It's okay, I don't mind' said Matt, stroking the damp fur. He liked dogs and would love to have one of his own. Unfortunately, his grandad was allergic to them, so there was no chance of that. As it was he would have to brush any residue of dog hair off of his clothes before he got home otherwise he would set his grandad off sneezing!

Zandi lapped up the attention for a few moments then was off, chasing another stick thrown by his owner. Matt was alone once more, but not for long.

There was a scuffling of feet behind him followed by sniggering. Matt knew even without looking that it was Fowler.

'Well look who's here' smirked Fowler 'if it isn't spider

legs'. Spider legs was the name which Fowler gave to Matt on account of him being tall and lanky.

Matt turned round slowly to face his enemy.

Fowler stood just a few feet away from him, his pale face reflecting the sun. He was accompanied by his two closest friends, Jack and Kenny.

'We saw you with your four legged friend' said Fowler, 'would you like to play fetch?' Jack and Kenny sniggered at this.

Matt remained silent, dreading what was coming next.

'I said would you like to play fetch?' Fowler inched closer.

Matt continued to say nothing, but stared back at Fowler his blue eyes intense.

'Perhaps he's gone deaf' suggested Kenny

'No, he's just playing hard to get' replied Jack.

All three boys sniggered and edged closer to Matt who stood his ground.

Fowler circled him, prodding him on the shoulder with one finger.

'I don't like being ignored' he said, 'Where's your manners freak?'

Matt felt the anger welling up inside him. It was as if the heat of the day was somehow being absorbed into his body.

'Didn't your parents teach you any – oh, but I forgot, they ran out on you didn't they?' This remark seemed to cut into Matt like a knife.

Fowler gestured to Kenny, 'find a suitable stick Ken'. He turned to face Matt. 'I'll teach you some manners'.

Matt felt his temperature rising so much, he was sure that at any time he would melt.

Kenny found a large stick and proceeded to give it to Fowler.

'Perfect' said Fowler running his hand up and down the stick. He looked at Matt menacingly.

'You're going to regret being so rude spider legs' he said, raising the stick above his head ready to strike Matt.

What happened next would shock them all.

Matt had no idea what was happening to him, but something inside seemed to take hold. It was almost as if an inner part of him was developing a life of its own, growing within him. In his mind he visualized the stick that Fowler was holding as a snake, then he directed this image at Fowler, Jack and Kenny. For a few moments there was no reaction and time seemed to stand still. Then it happened.

There was a loud shriek followed by a thud as the stick fell to the ground.

Fowler, Kenny and Jack stared at it in disbelief, their eyes seemed to be playing tricks on them. For, there on the ground, where the stick had been, was a large snake, writhing around.

At first they didn't move, frozen with fear. Then, the snake hissed, causing them to jump back.

'Oh my god!' shrieked Fowler.

Matt watched as the three bullies cowered in front of him, suddenly they didn't look so menacing anymore. He found himself strangely calmed by this. Somehow he knew that he was now the one in control of the situation. The snake wasn't real, he knew it, it was all in their minds and he was making them see it. He didn't know how he was doing it - all he knew was that he was. Somehow he had managed to infiltrate their minds and control what they saw. From that moment on Matt knew things were going to be different and what was happening was just the beginning.

'Let's get out of here' yelled Kenny.

Matt remained silent as the three boys turned and ran for their lives. Shortly after they had gone, he looked down at the snake, but it had gone and all that remained was a large stick.

Matt didn't say anything about the incident to his grandad when he arrived home. He didn't suppose he would believe him anyway.

Because it was a Friday Matt and his grandad had fish and chips, a tradition that had survived throughout the years. Then, after they had eaten they went for a walk to work it off.

Because it was such a hot evening they decided to walk towards Tipton following the path of the river Otter, eventually stopping by the rocky weir, where grandad could rest his 'weary bones' as he put it. They sat watching the water cascade down the rocks and Matt was able to relax and forget about the events of the day. The evening sun looked like a giant orange globe in the cloudless summer sky and the sound of sea gulls filled the air. It was moments like this that Matt wished he could hold onto forever. He looked at his grandad's face, lined by years of exposure to the elements, his tanned skin was framed by a shock of pure white hair. He had the same intense blue eyes as Matt. Matt had no idea how old he was because everybody over 16 looked old to him, but he guessed he had to be at least sixty and to Matt that seemed very old! Even though he was aware that there were people around those days who were over a hundred, he still worried that his grandad would die before he grew up.

'A penny for your thoughts' his grandad asked him, interrupting the silence.

'I was just thinking about mum and dad' replied Matt, 'wondering what really happened to them and where they are now'.

'Ah' said his grandad, 'I often do that too'.

'Do you think they will ever come back?' Matt asked.

His grandad sighed before replying, 'I don't know Matt, but I pray every day that they will'.

He looked down at the small face that was full of concern. Sometimes he could see his son (Matt's dad) in him. He had the same blue eyes and mass of dark hair as his dad. A pang of sadness came over him as he thought about his son's strange disappearance. A mystery never to be solved, so it seemed, for what exactly happened on that day nobody seemed to know.

As if reading his thoughts Matt said, 'Tell me again what happened on the day they disappeared grandad', even though his grandad had told him many times before, he still needed to hear it again, hoping that he would understand a bit more each time.

'Okay, Matt' said his grandad, reluctantly, for he found it painful to revisit that episode in time.

'The gist of it is that your mum and dad went on a boating trip with some friends. It was a fine summer's day and the water was as calm as a mill pond because there was virtually no wind. They set off from the marina at Exmouth intending to drop anchor by a cove near Ladrum Bay that was only accessible by boat, however they never arrived at their destination, nor did they ever return, and despite a thorough search being carried out by sea and air, neither the boat or their bodies were ever

The Present Future

discovered. It was a complete mystery. Both your mum and dad were strong swimmers and your dad had been a Marine for many years, which meant that he was well equipped to cope with any adverse conditions which might occur. Yet nothing out of the ordinary had been reported that day. There were no sudden changes in the weather and no sightings of whales, or submarines or anything which might have caused them to have a collision and, in any event, no wreckage was found. After six months had passed and they failed to turn up, they were presumed dead and it was just you and me from then on' his grandad smiled at him.

Matt listened carefully to every word his grandad said, his young mind trying, but failing, to find the answers. He loved his grandad and though he was now the only family he had left, Matt always believed that his parents were still alive and would turn up one day.

Matt's grandad wished that he could have done more. He had done his best for the lad but it wasn't the same. It would have been better had his dear wife still been alive, but sadly she died when Matt was only two. It was up to Matt now to continue the family line, and what a burden that would be! He wondered how long it would be before Matt discovered the family gift if you could call it that, he had battled with it over the years, not knowing whether it was in fact a gift or a curse. His son had managed to avoid it, since it always seemed to skip a generation, which meant that it was sure to pass on to Matt. He only hoped he was there to smooth the way for him when it happened.

'Hadn't we better be going now' said Matt as dusk started to fall.

'Yes, you're right' replied his grandad, 'we should

make it back just before dark'. So, on that note the two of them stood up and headed back along the river towards Ottery.

The river took on an eerie look as the sunlight began to fade and Matt could have sworn there were shadowy figures lurking behind the trees, waiting to pounce. However, there was not a soul about other than the two of them and some cows laying down in a huddle, making the most of the cooling evening air. Soon they could see the lights from the houses overlooking the river and Matt felt relieved to be getting nearer to home. As they reached the bridge just a short distance from the houses, darkness descended making the water look like black oil. They were just about to cross the bridge when a hooded figure appeared in front of them making them both jump.

'Good evening' said the hooded man, his face partially hidden, 'can you spare me some credit?

'Sorry mate we haven't got any' replied his grandad.

The hooded man looked down at him, there was something very sinister about his demeanour.

'I'll settle for the time piece then' he said menacingly, gesturing towards his grandad's watch.

'You've got to be joking' said his grandad, 'it's a family heirloom, there's no way I'd part with it'.

The hooded man wasn't going to give up easily and much to Matt's horror he produced a knife and pointed it at his grandad.

'I'm not afraid to use this' he said between clenched teeth, 'now give it over'.

Matt's grandad didn't budge. The hooded man edged closer to them and Matt felt his heart rate increase. He didn't want anything to happen to his grandad, he refused to stand by and see him getting hurt. He remembered what he had done to Rick Fowler and his mates earlier on that afternoon and wondered if he could repeat the performance.

'I said give it over!' the hooded man was beginning to lose patience, he'd show the old man who was boss. He was on the run from a murder charge so had nothing to lose. He would strike quickly, slash the old man, grab the watch and disappear. He went to lurch at the old man, but suddenly found he couldn't move, his feet seemed to be glued to the ground. *What the hell!* he looked down at them. He couldn't understand it, why wouldn't his feet move? It was hard to see with the darkness but he could just about make out that his feet were sinking into what seemed to be boggy ground. He tried to lift his legs, first one, then the other, but to no avail. The more he tried to lift them the further he sank into the ground. He began to panic.

'Help me I'm sinking' he yelled at Matt's grandad, who was completely baffled by what was happening. All he could see was the man swaying around like a drunk. The man looked down, he was now waist deep in the bog, if he didn't get out soon, it would swallow him up completely.

'Please, you've got to help me man!' he shrieked in desperation.

Matt's grandad couldn't understand, one minute this hooded man had been threatening to stab him with a knife, then all of a sudden he seemed to be overcome by something, some strange kind of paralysis. Whatever it was he felt no sympathy for him and decided that it would be a good opportunity for them to make a swift exit.

He looked at Matt who was staring at the man, his

eyes fixed firmly on him, full of concentration. It was at that moment that he knew.

'Come on Matt, lets go' he urged his grandson, grabbing his hand.

Matt's concentration was broken, and the hooded man, who had started to say his prayers, suddenly found that he was free from the bog. However, he was so freaked out by what had happened that he no longer cared about the watch any more, he just wanted to get out of there and scarpered leaving Matt and his grandad behind.

When they got home, Matt's grandad knew what he must do. He sat Matt down with a mug of hot chocolate and told Matt what he had been told by his own grandad when he first discovered he had the gift.

'Matt' he said looking into his grandson's eyes 'you are a very clever and sensible child and that's why I know you will heed what I am about to tell you'.

Matt looked at him, wondering what he was going to say next.

'What happened tonight to that man was your doing wasn't it?

Matt nodded his head, afraid to speak.

'Matt what you have is a gift, a family gift passed on to you as it was to me', His grandad started to explain, *how he had dreaded this moment.*

'We don't know exactly what it is, but the story goes that a special gene exists within our family a gene that is passed on to male members only'.

'What's a gene?' asked Matt, finally finding his tongue.

'A gene is part of what makes us who we are' his grandad replied, trying to find a simple way of explaining human genetics. 'We all have many different genes in our bodies, each playing an important role in our physical development, our individual characteristics and personalities. This particular gene I am talking about gives us special abilities, abilities to get inside the minds of other people, to make them see, hear and feel things which aren't real, things that could potentially harm them if used wrongly'.

Matt could sense that his grandad was getting serious now.

'I know it's hard for you to take in Matt, but remember this, you must only ever use your gift as a shield and not a sword.'

Matt stared back at the wise face, comforted, but at the same time freaked out by what he was hearing.

'Matt, you must never use your gift to do harm to others unless it is absolutely necessary, do you understand?

Matt nodded and continued to sip his hot chocolate as his grandad passed on his knowledge and words of wisdom. So began the beginning of a journey, one which would take him further than he could ever have imagined possible.

CHAPTER TWO

KINGS SCHOOL, OTTERY ST MARY, TWENTY YEARS LATER

MATT JACOBS ADDRESSED HIS CLASS.
'This term we are going to be studying the early part of the 21st century?' he said looking around at the sea of faces. 'Can anybody tell me of a significant event that marked the beginning of that era?' He was met with silence. This did not deter him since it was often the case on the first day of a new term.

'Okay' he smiled, 'let me give you a few clues'. He activated the central viewing pod and the holographic simulator sprang to life. The class watched as images of events which had occurred long before they were born were played out all around them in 3D. They saw a giant hollow cylinder housing what looked like a spiral metal vein filled with white glowing plasma.

'What you are seeing now is the advent of nuclear fusion as an alternative energy provider. In the year two thousand and twenty seven, power stations which used fossil fuels were finally abandoned in favour of those using a sustainable, renewable energy system which didn't harm the environment.'

They watched as this image was replaced with one of a monorail track raised high in the sky, with trains floating above it and bombing along at great speed.

'In two thousand and forty nine the world's transport systems were dramatically changed.' Matt continued with the narrative. 'The era of the superconductor track had begun. All trains ran on tracks made of magnetised ceramic which effectively repelled them along, dispensing with the need to use fossil fuel driven engines. This eventually resulted in new roads being built, using the same principal and cars with fossil fuel driven piston engines gradually became obsolete replaced with those driven by the force of magnetism, such as we have today.'

The holographic simulator then showed a large jet taking off and flying over the heads of the students. It was so realistic that some of them ducked in fear.

'The technology for aircraft and boats also moved on' Matt continued, 'Their engines were adapted so that they could run using solid molybdenum, a silver white metallic element which generated enough power to drive them without the need to refuel as often as they had done using fossil fuel, making them more efficient and less harmful to the environment'.

Matt could sense his class getting distracted, he would throw in a question to regain their attention.

'By the end of two thousand and sixty, vehicles with piston engines were largely confined to museums or private collections. There was a big impact on the world economy. What do you think happened to those nations that relied on fossil fuels as a main source of income?'

Matt stopped the holographic simulator and scanned the faces of his students to look for any raised hands.

There were three. 'much more encouraging' he thought.

'Okay Caitlin tell me your thoughts on this' he addressed a young fair haired girl who was gazing at him admiringly. She had a mega crush on him. Her freckled face went pink as he looked her in the eye and she found herself blushing.

'They collapsed and became impoverished' she managed to say.

Matt paused before responding.

'Yes, Caitlin that's more or less what happened. It was a clear reversal of fortune. They went from being the richest nations in the world to the poorest, having to rely on tourism for survival'.

At that point the buzzer for the morning break sounded.

'Okay guys, time to take a break for a while, but make sure you're back in half an hour' Matt told his class and they all sauntered out chatting among themselves.

Matt walked out of the classroom without realising that he had left his communicator behind. It was swiftly retrieved by Caitlin Simmons, much to the horror of her best friend Michaela.

'You are going to hand it in straight away aren't you?' Michaela quizzed her besotted friend.

'Of course' came the response, 'well before the start of the next lesson anyway. I'm sure he won't miss it until then' she beamed. Michaela watched with concern as Caitlin accessed the communicator searching its files for what, she dreaded to think.

Matt retreated to the staff room for a few moments peace before the next lesson began. He was annoyed to find Ron Brown drinking a cup of tea out of his mug. Ron was well known for using other people's mugs, a habit which intensely annoyed the other members of staff including Matt. So Matt decided to teach him a lesson.

'Hi Ron' he said jovially.

'Oh, hi Matt' replied Ron, his big red moustache covered in what looked like biscuit crumbs. *Oh joy* thought Matt, now he would have to disinfect the mug.

'Ron, what's that on the side of your mug?' he asked, failing to mention that it was his mug Ron was using.

'Uh?' said Ron, looking to see what Matt was talking about.

'Holey sponges!' he exclaimed, nearly choking on his biscuit. His piggy like eyes stared at the mug in horror. For there, crawling up the side was a big fat slimy slug.

'Ugh!' he said in disgust before throwing the mug into the sink. 'How in God's name did that get there?'

Matt struggled to refrain from laughing.

'What do you mean?' Matt asked.

'That slug, you know, the one you so kindly pointed out' replied Ron, a slight annoyance in his tone.

'What slug?' teased Matt, 'I was merely referring to what looked like a big blob of jam from your biscuit'.

Ron pointed to the mug, 'look see for yourself'.

Matt looked at the spilt mug in the sink, knowing full well that there was no slug since he had created the illusion himself.

'I can't see a slug Ron, are you sure that was tea you were drinking?' he teased.

Ron was getting agitated.

'ARE YOU PLAYING GAMES WITH ME JACOBS?' he said with a raised voice, however, when he looked at the sink he could no longer see a slug, only the mug and its spilt contents. He was momentarily dumb struck, *surely he couldn't have imagined it?*

'It was there I'm telling you' he said, feeling deflated. There was something about Matt Jacobs that he didn't like, he was smug, that was it! The slug had been there, he knew it, it must have crawled away.

'Yeah, yeah Ron' said Matt, 'I believe you thought you saw a slug, but clearly it's not there now, so if I was you I'd use less gin next time'. Ron's piggy eyes looked as though they would burst after hearing Matt's intimidating words, he glared at him. *Time to make a sharp exit* thought Matt.

'No worries, Ron, I've got to dash' were his parting words. Outside the staff room he couldn't resist chuckling to himself.

A short while later the second lesson began and the class reassembled. Caitlin casually put the stolen communicator back before Matt noticed that it had gone. She had devoured its contents in the girls toilets during break and couldn't wait to tell Michaela what she had learned from it, but that would have to wait until the end of class.

Matt continued with his history lecture.

'There were many other great discoveries in the 21st century' he said, scanning them all to make sure they were concentrating.

'including great advances in medicine. It was the geneticists of the 21st century who paved the way to using stem cell technology to grow new organs, limbs and spinal chords. Physicists developed nanotechnology, enabling repairs to be carried out inside the human body by microscopic robots.'

'Not to mention Professor Henry Pinkerton, my personal favourite of all the protagonists of the new era'. He paused for thought. 'Ah, but that will have to wait until next time' he smiled at them.

'For the rest of the lesson I would like you all to study the section on the era of sustainable, renewable energy, which can be found in your personal holopods. I will be grilling you on it tomorrow'.

Each student then put on their headsets and withdrew into their virtual reality holopods of learning.

Matt kept a watchful eye on them, making sure they weren't skipping into Music World or one of the many gaming planets. His thoughts were interrupted by a request for assistance from one of his students.

'Sir, could you please look at my holopod, I can't seem to make it work'.

He looked up to see the request was coming from Caitlin Simmons. He got up and went over to her work station.

'What seems to be the problem?' he asked, scrutinizing her with his deep blue eyes.

'I don't know, the image keeps jamming for some reason' was her flustered reply.

'Let me have a look' Matt smiled, gesturing for her to move aside so that he could examine the device. Caitlin slid off of her seat and stood behind him as he tried to find out what was wrong. She watched as he fiddled with the controls, bringing up images of a bygone world as the holopod played out its contents list. However, when he selected the appropriate programme, it started to falter after a few seconds and the image froze and started flickering. He frowned, unable to figure out the cause.

'It's no good, I'll have to get IT to come and have a look at it' he sighed. Technology wasn't his strong point, a fact that Caitlin was well aware of when she created the fault. She couldn't resist it! Just a few brief minutes of his undivided attention was all she needed to get her fix for the day. Matt got up and sent a help request text to IT on his communicator. Caitlin resumed her seat, relishing the warm spot from where he had been sitting.

Michaela, was not amused. She knew that Caitlin

had deliberately sabotaged the holopod. 'One of these days you'll get caught out' she hissed. Caitlin smiled, she didn't care.

As usual IT didn't turn up until the end of the lesson and Caitlin had to share Michaela's holopod as there wasn't a spare one available. The school operated on a very tight budget.

Towards the end of the lesson Matt turned off the holopods to discuss an important topic, the time capsule project.

'Okay everybody can I have your attention please, we have something important to do this week. No doubt you will all have heard of the time capsule project. This year our school has been given the opportunity to take part in the project which is carried out every fifty years by the Science Council of East Devon. We have been asked to provide memorabilia of life in the year twenty one eleven. The memorabilia is to include items commonly used in every day life and recordings made by students, giving a brief insight into their lives. The memorabilia and recordings will then be placed in a metal capsule, sealed and buried underground, to be retrieved in many years to come by a future generation. So what I want each of you to do is to take a holopod home with you and make a recording of your life, including your hobbies and interests, things you like, pet hates and anything you think will be of interest to future generations. Please refrain from using obscenities, as these will be edited out and the relevant culprits disciplined!' The class laughed at this comment.

'Now, does anybody have any questions about this?'

One hand was raised in the air.

'Yes, Michaela?' Matt prompted.

'How long has the recording got to be?' Michaela asked

'Good point. Roughly ten minutes should suffice, though it doesn't matter if you do slightly more or less since each recording will be edited and merged into one. It's entirely up to you how you do it. You can do a monologue or interview other members of your family as you see fit. This is your opportunity to be creative, so create your masterpiece!'.

On that note the buzzer indicating the end of class sounded and the students started to disperse. Matt flexed his hands ready to go and teach the next bunch of 'eager to learn' students. He wondered why had he let himself be persuaded into teaching teenagers in his sleepy home town, when he could have accepted one of the many offers to be a research fellow at some of the most prestigious universities in Europe. His knowledge of the human psyche was second to none and he had written several books on the subject as well as being invited to give lectures all over Europe. So why had he ended up here? The answer of course was because of his wife Jen. She had encouraged him to take that road, enthusing about the benefits of helping young minds to develop. He remembered the conversation they had had when he returned from his year long sabbatical touring Europe with the occasional lecture at one or two universities on the way.

'Matt' Jen said, fixing her brown eyes intently on him, 'you are one of the best teachers I know. You have the ability to make even the most dry, uninteresting topics come to life. Just think of the lives you could change, the futures you could shape. You have such a talent for nurturing young minds, why waste it?' She smiled at him.

'I wish you'd consider taking the post at King's school, even if it's only for a couple of years'. Matt looked at his wife, her pixie like face was framed by short wispy golden hair which over emphasised her large brown eyes. He always found it hard to say no to her.

'How can I possibly argue with that' he replied.

Jen grinned, 'you're a push over really' she added. They both laughed and Jen marvelled at how lucky she was to have found her soul mate so early on in life. They met when they were both ten and bonded almost instantly. They were like two peas in a pod, inseparable, sometimes Jen felt there was almost a telepathy between them. She remembered how as children they would love to take their bikes to the woods at East Hill and, on one particular occasion, she had panicked when she got lost. She kept calling to Matt for what seemed like an eternity and she could have sworn that she heard his voice in her head, calming her down and telling her not to worry, he would find her, all she had to do was focus on some identifiable landmark near to where she was. So she stared at a large pine tree that stood out from the rest due to its sheer enormity, and before long Matt was at her side. For some reason the telepathy was never discussed, maybe because they were children and just accepted it. Maybe it was just coincidence that he found her and the rest was her imagination.

Whatever, she was glad she stuck with the lanky lad with floppy hair, despite her friends telling her she could have done better, as she loved him with all her heart and knew he was the one for her. It wasn't long before the lad became an Adonis and all her friends envied her. He had a mop of dark brown hair that made you want to run your

The Present Future

fingers through it and chiselled features set off perfectly by the bluest eyes on the planet. Yes, she was the lucky one.

Matt often felt that Jen could have been a politician had she not chosen to be a scientist, since she had tremendous powers of persuasion. Because of this he ended up at Kings School, teaching 11 - 18 year olds. However, it had not all been in vain, he had to admit that he enjoyed it, and most of his students passed their higher levels with flying colours.

Matt felt a pang of sadness when he thought about Jen. At that moment in time she was further away from him than she had ever been before.

Jen was a research scientist with a particular interest in space travel. She had responded to an advertisement in New Age Science magazine inviting 'Earth bound' readers to apply to take part in the maiden voyage of the new Super Vulcan, so named because of its resemblance to the old British bomber jet which had a brief life in the twentieth century. However, this was where the similarity ended, for the Super Vulcan was no bomber jet, it was a spacecraft powered using the latest solar technology. Its large triangular shaped wings were fitted with lightweight panels made from reflective material which acted like giant energy cells capturing the sun's rays and generating enough power to drive its engines through space. It was much lighter and faster than its predecessors, plus it could travel for an infinite amount of time, covering great distances, without having to stop to refuel. It had been designed so that it could be launched from land or sea and could land vertically, thus requiring little space to manoeuvre. This was an opportunity Jen could not resist. So she sent her application in, was invited to attend an interview and, having competed against thousands of equally keen candidates from all over the world, was delighted to be the successful one. Matt wasn't at all surprised by this but was more than a little concerned for her safety. He took little comfort in her assurances that the astronaut in command was one of the best there was and that she would be back in no time. However, he accepted that this was the opportunity of a lifetime for Jen, and far be it for him to deny her the chance to achieve her dream. So he had reluctantly agreed that she should give it a go.

In their two years of marriage, they had scarcely spent a single night apart, so he was going to miss her terribly.

He had listened intently to her tales of the gruelling training programme and told her not to despair when she felt she could not make the grade. He had delighted in her exhilaration when she passed the rigorous tests with the ease of a pro and had gone with her to watch her depart on the biggest adventure of her life. She would be gone for three months, a long time for them to be apart. So he travelled with her to the space elevator, to see her off.

The space elevator was an awesome structure, one of mankind's greatest feats of engineering, extending 22,000 miles above the earth into geostationary orbit. It consisted of 4 cables made from carbon nanotubes, 10 times stronger than steel but much lighter and more flexible and strong enough to withstand the forces of nature. Each cable carried either passenger pods, or equipment. Altogether there were 3 space elevators across the World. The first had been constructed in 2050 at the Kennedy Space Centre, Cape Canaveral in the USA. The other two had been constructed at later dates, one in England and the other in Australia, both were completed by 2070. The elevators had made space travel far more economical and practical.

The Present Future

Space shuttles could dock at the elevators, refuel, accept payloads, and have routine maintenance carried out on them, without the need to return to Earth very often.

The Super Vulcan was currently docked at the elevator in London, England where it was being loaded up with equipment and supplies for the journey. This was where Jen would join the rest of the crew ready for departure.

Saying goodbye was the hardest part for Matt. Second to that was watching her go.

'Are you sure about this Jen?' he asked, even though he already knew the answer.

'Positive' she replied, trying to hide her nerves. How she would miss him, but there was no going back now, she had come this far. They gave each other one last kiss before Jen entered the passenger pod.

Matt stood with the other relatives of the crew in the viewing station and watched as the passenger pod began its journey up the track of the space elevator. It would take 24 hours to reach the top. In the early days before high speed superconductor tracks were developed the journey would have taken 5 days.

Matt suddenly felt very alone, his soul mate had departed on a journey taking her way beyond the reach of conventional transport. He hoped nothing would go wrong.

The Super Vulcan was primed and ready to depart from the docking station at the top of the elevator. For the first week after departure it was to orbit the earth and make regular pit stops at each space elevator to check that everything was in working order before beginning its journey into deep space.

Jen transmitted regular messages to Matt, reassuring him that everything was going smoothly and she had suffered no ill effects to date. In addition to this, he had discovered as much as he could about the other members of the crew, and they were, it seemed, the cream of the crop. Jack Simmons, was the astronaut in command and he had completed 10 missions, one of them to Mars. His second in command, Bob Gilmore, had been an astronaut for 5 years and had accompanied Jack on several missions. The rest of the crew members were made up of renowned scientists and highly qualified engineers from all over the world. Matt was sure Jen was in safe hands, however, he was going to miss her and would be glad when she returned safe and sound. He only had a few more days when he could remain in contact with her, after that, once they departed into deep space they would be out of range of contact via personal communication equipment and he would be reliant on messages sent from the space mission. That was the bit he dreaded, the day she embarked on a journey into the unknown. Matt sighed, bringing himself back to the present, 'roll on three months', he said to himself, time couldn't go quickly enough for him.

Caitlin and Michaela sat eating their lunch in the local park, escaping from the school grounds for a while. Caitlin took a great delight in telling her friend what she had found out whilst rifling through Mr Jacob's communicator,

'Hey you'll never guess what I found out about Mr Jacobs' she said

'Like I care' sighed Michaela, 'so what is it, pray tell me?' she relented.

'Well, the bad news is that he's married to a woman called Jen, but the good news is; you'll never believe this' she said excitedly.

'Go on, do tell before I die of boredom' urged Michaela.

'By an incredible coincidence she is one of the crew of the Super Vulcan, you know the new shuttle thingy that dad is piloting, cool yeah'.

Michaela was not amused.

'So why is that such good news?' she asked.

'Because the Super Vulcan will soon depart into deep space and be gone for three months and Mr Jacobs will be alone which means I'll be in with a chance!'

'I think you're really sad' smirked Michaela, she knew nothing good would come of it.

CHAPTER THREE

That evening Caitlin decided to make her recording for the time capsule project. She adjusted her long fair hair and checked her reflection in the mirror before starting, she had to look just right. Then, turning to face the camera on the holopod, she took a deep breath, smiled, selected record and began speaking into the mike.

'Hi, my name is Caitlin Simmons. The date is the 7th of September twenty one eleven and this is my entry for the time capsule project'. She paused the holopod and pressed replay to check the recording. Her face looked different, slightly distorted somehow, but then she was used to seeing herself in mirror vision, and, was that really her voice? How flat it sounded.

She continued with her recording trying to add musical tones to her vocals to make it more interesting.

'Today is a very special day. Not only is it my sixteenth birthday, but it is also my great grandmother's birthday and she is one hundred and sixteen! Can you believe that? She has been alive one hundred years longer than me!'
How stupid did she sound?

' We are having a joint party to celebrate on Saturday and since the local climate control office has confirmed that it will be a warm sunny day, we can have the party outside. That's assuming that climate control don't make any mistakes with their weather planning, which they have been known to do on odd occasions. Who knows, we could be in for a thunderstorm instead, ha ha ha!'

She took in a deep breath and continued.

'Great Gran can remember the days before they could control the climate. She was born in 1995. Can you believe that before the days of climate control they had to guess what the weather was going to be like, making forecasts based on readings taken from machines that measured the wind, temperature, pressure and humidity! These forecasts were not very reliable and often wrong. Great Gran told me that on one occasion they were completely off the mark, so much so that a great disaster was to follow. Instead of the mild winds predicted, there was a great hurricane, destroying hundreds of homes and changing the shape of the landscape beyond all recognition in some parts of the South East. This became known as the great storm'.

Caitlin could not imagine what it must have been like back then.

'Thankfully, by the year two thousand and fifty meteorologists discovered how to manipulate the weather systems across the world and climate control was born. The climate could be adjusted so as to ensure exactly the right amount of sunshine and rainfall to maintain a healthy planet. Being able to control the weather had a big impact on the world's ecology. Meteorologists were able to eradicate hurricanes and tornadoes and prevent flooding and droughts'.

Enough of that she thought. Would people in the future really be interested in the weather? The truth was she was only trying to impress Mr Jacobs with her in depth knowledge of meteorology.

So, she moved onto the mundane subject of every day life, like she was supposed to.

'I have one sister, Tamara aged twelve and a brother,

Gavin aged ten. That makes me the eldest. Great Gran Mel also lives with us in the annexe. What else can I tell you, um, we live 6 miles from the sea in a small town called Ottery St Mary with nothing much going on', she paused for thought. Her life really sucked didn't it?

She continued, 'My dad has a really cool career, he's an astronaut and at this present moment in time is orbiting the earth in the Super Vulcan, an awesome new spacecraft. He'll be gone for a few months exploring deep space, away from this place, lucky man' She stopped recording, that was the bit that would really impress Mr Jacobs, he would learn that her dad was the captain of the Super Vulcan and, with a bit of luck, that would buy her more precious time in his company.

'Caitlin?' her mother called from downstairs. 'Dinner's ready'. That was her cue to call it a day.

She went downstairs and was pleased to see that her great gran Mel was joining them for dinner that evening. It was a rare thing since she was very finicky about her food preferring her own youth preserving concoctions. Mind you Caitlin had to admit they seemed to work, Mel was extremely fit and supple for her age and was always keen to prove that she could still touch her toes, plus her teeth were all her own, and she still had a good head of hair. She was already sitting at the table, sipping a glass of blue liquid.

'What on earth is that GG? Caitlin asked her (GG was her pet name for her).

'Youth preserving serum' replied Mel, 'it keeps me fit and healthy'.

Caitlin sat down next to her, she was fascinated by her. They had a bond between them that was almost stronger than the one between her and her mum. Ever since she could remember Caitlin had spent many an hour listening to Mel talk about her past and the way life used to be in the dark ages as she called them. She loved to look at the old digital photos of family members she had never met since they had long since died including Mel's husband Sam (her great grandfather). She remembered how once she had said to Mel 'I wish I could have met Sam' and Mel looked at her with a strange twinkle in her eye and said 'one day you will'. This puzzled Caitlin since Mel wasn't particularly religious and she couldn't imagine that she meant in the afterlife, so what did she mean? Mel would never say anything further other than 'just wait and see'.

On that particular evening Mel seemed energized, she was looking forward to their forthcoming joint party immensely.

'I'll need to get a new dress to wear' she said, 'I can't possibly be seen in the same one I wore to the last party, whenever that was', she strained to think of the last time she went to a party. When you got to her age the endless years of partying behind you all tended to merge into one, and birthdays, well, they were best forgotten about! Though there was always one that she remembered vividly more than the others, and that was a special one, when she turned sixteen. That was the year she finally grew up and discovered that there was more to life than she could ever have imagined, plus there was an unexpected guest that year, she looked at Caitlin and smiled.

'One day Cait' she said softly, 'one day'.

Caitlin smiled at her, not having a clue what she meant.

The rest of the week at school seemed to go by in a bit of a haze and Caitlin could not help but notice that Mr Jacobs was a bit distracted. The recordings they had all made for the time capsule project were edited and merged together ready for the big event on Friday. Caitlin wondered if Mr Jacobs had been impressed by her recording and was hoping he might make a point of mentioning it, however, he didn't. He hadn't even acknowledged that Jack Simmons, the astronaut, was her father. It transpired that he had not been involved in editing and merging the recording at all, IT had done it all. He just congratulated them all on a job well done and left it at that.

Friday arrived and a small crowd gathered at the Land of Canaan in Ottery St. Mary to witness the burial of the time capsule. The air was electric with excitement. Dozens of airborne holopods frantically swerved to avoid colliding with each other. The ceremony was to be conducted by the Chairman of the Science Council. In attendance was a selection of pupils from the Kings School led by Matt Jacobs. Two of the students were Caitlin and Michaela. The rest of the crowd was made up of Science Council members.

The buzzing crowd was hushed by the arrival of the Chairman as he emerged from his chauffeur driven vehicle. He was a fairly stout man and looked as if he had been shoe-horned into his tunic. He took several steps forward to the specially erected rostrum, then mounted it and turned to face the small crowd.

'Ladies and gentlemen' he addressed them. 'Welcome to this exciting event. Today is a very special one, for today we bury the time capsule filled with memorabilia from the year twenty one eleven. Who knows what a future generation will make of us. Will they look at us with admiration, or regard us with disdain? Perhaps they will simply find our lifestyles of great amusement, as we found those of the generations who lived before us. Who can say? What's important is that so many members of the community have given their support to this project, contributing items that mean a lot to them and give an insight into their every day lives. This is most admirable and I would like to thank you all for your contribution and for being here today'.

The crowd burst into applause.

'I would like to give special thanks to the pupils of Kings school, some of whom are here today'. He gestured in the direction of the lucky students who had been selected to represent their school. 'They all got together and made a recording depicting life as it is today and this has been included in the capsule,' the crowd applauded again and the students grimaced with embarrassment.

'And now, without further ado, let the ceremony begin' he pressed the button and the apparatus before him sprang into action. The small capsule was lifted over a hole in the ground by a robotic arm, then gently lowered in. Once safely deposited, the robotic arm filled in the hole with earth and placed a shiny stone plaque on top. Following this, the robotic arm produced a metal box, opened it and a flock of brightly coloured robotic birds burst out, flying high into the sky, spelling out the words 'time capsule twenty one eleven'

The crowd cheered at this display, then went to collect their complimentary glasses of champagne and canapés. Matt instructed his students that they were free to enjoy the rest of the afternoon as they wished and turned to make his exit. He had no wish to join in the celebrations.

Caitlin and her best friend Michaela decided to go shopping, tomorrow was Saturday the day of the big party and their mission was to find something for Caitlin to wear.

'You need something that will make an impact' said Michaela.

Caitlin grimaced 'I couldn't make an impact if I turned up naked' she said.

'You are most definitely wrong!' said Michaela, 'and I intend to prove it. Come on lets go, we still have a few hours until closing time, thanks to Mr Jacobs letting us have the afternoon off'.

The two girls took the silver sky tram to the Alpine village. The Alpine village had been constructed at the end of the previous year on the site of what used to be a business park which had long fallen into a state of disrepair and had become a real eyesore. So the business park was abolished and replaced with the Alpine village, a new concept in modern living which, in addition to lots of lovely shops, contained leisure facilities, including lakes and outdoor ski slopes. The village was modelled very much on an alpine ski resort, hence the name, and in the winter months, snow was created by climate control ensuring a persistent white covering over everything to give it an air of authenticity and to enable skiers to practice their moves on the small artificial slopes. In the summer it was very much café culture, the cobbled streets were littered with little bistros with tables and chairs outside where you could bask in the sun, take a dip in one of the lakes, or take refuge under a large sunshade whilst sipping your favourite iced drink. There was no traffic permitted in the village, other than the delivery vehicles. Customers had to get around on foot or bicycle. They were transported to and from the village by the sky tram.

Caitlin and Michaela loved it there, it was where they

spent the majority of their spare time. Caitlin had received credits from her mum and GG as a birthday present and was going to use these to buy herself something new to wear for the party on Saturday. Michaela hoped it would take her mind off of the object of her affection, Mr Jacobs! Though she could see the attraction, she preferred guys of her own age. She sometimes felt that Caitlin's obsession was due to the fact that she needed a father figure, since her dad was hardly ever home, with him being an astronaut.

The two girls hit the shops with a fury and after trying on countless clothes, of varying combinations, Caitlin finally settled on a pair of pink Lyntex trousers with a matching sleeveless top and some slinky cream coloured ankle boots. Michaela told her that 'she looked the part' and the pair sat down outside one of the many bistros to rest their weary feet and drink ice cold fruit juices. Whilst they were there the central viewing pod started transmitting pictures of the time capsule burial from earlier that day. Caitlin and Michaela were ecstatic to see themselves in one of the shots, Michaela's jet black hair and olive skin contrasted strongly against Caitlin's fair hair and freckled complexion.

'Look, we're famous' said Michaela.

They watched the viewing pod play out the event. It was interesting to be able to see views that they hadn't been able to see themselves when they were there due to the crowd being in the way. There was one shot , however, that caused Caitlin's heart to skip a beat, the holopod had scanned the crowd and focussed on Mr Jacobs, his gorgeous face was there on the giant screen staring right at her. She felt like she'd died and gone to heaven. Michaela tutted

'Oh, please!' she muttered under her breath.

'Come on' she nudged her star struck pal 'let's make tracks, it's getting late'. Reluctantly Caitlin got up and followed Michaela back to the tram stop.

CHAPTER FOUR

Saturday arrived warm, bright and sunny. Climate control had not let them down. It was going to be a perfect day for a party. Karel Simmons, Caitlin's mum, was relieved. A good party was something they all needed. She had pulled out all the stops to make sure that it was going to be a day that her eldest daughter and Mel, her grandmother would remember. Mel had taken over the role of mother to Karel when she was six years old when Karel's mother ran off with a neighbour and went to live in Australia. There had been little contact between Karel and her mother over the years and she showed no interest in meeting her grand children. So Mel had become the rock on which they all relied for many years, and now it was time to pay back her kindness and devotion.

So Karel was hosting a spectacular party for Mel and Caitlin to celebrate their joint birthdays. Luckily they had a big garden with room to accommodate all the guests. She had borrowed garden furniture from friends and neighbours and employed outside caterers to do the food for her. It was to be an afternoon event so that all ages could attend from small children to the elderly. There would be plenty of champagne and cocktails to keep everybody lubricated. She had even bought a new dress for the occasion with shoes to match. She just hoped that everybody would enjoy themselves. Tamara and Gavin, Caitlin's younger siblings, would do their best to keep the younger guests entertained. Tamara loved looking after children; Karel sometimes forgot she was still only a child herself. In some ways she was more mature than her elder sister Caitlin. Karel sighed at the thought. Caitlin – what was she going to do with her? She seemed to spend her time in a permanent haze, shut away in her bedroom, losing herself in some virtual reality programme no doubt! If only Jack, her father was there more often. He was away so frequently that Caitlin hardly knew him. However, when he was around he seemed to have a stabilising influence on her. It was just so typical that he wasn't there for her birthday – oh why had she chosen to marry an astronaut? She looked at his smiling photo on the fridge.

'If only you could be here' she said. 'Jack, what am I going to do with Caitlin?'

'Karel' she heard a male voice behind her. She swung round to see her neighbour Brian carrying a folded chair. 'I thought you could use a few more of these. Where would you like me to put them?'

'Oh, thank you Brian. If you could take them outside and put them with the others, that would be most helpful' she beamed at him, hoping that he hadn't heard her talking to Jack's photo.

As Brian took the chairs outside, a young woman with a box shaped bag arrived. It was Jane the mobile hairdresser and beautician, she had come to do the make-up and hair of the ladies of the house so that they would all look special for the event.

'Hi Karel, who wants to be transformed first?' she grinned, her teeth all perfectly white and even.

'Oh, I think Grandma Mel should be the first. She is over in the annex Jane, I think you know the way by now' she gestured for her to go to where the matriarch was eagerly waiting. Jane headed over to the annex, and Karel went to find Caitlin, she hoped that Jane would be able to magically transform her personality as well as her hair!

Caitlin was in her bedroom with Michaela. She didn't feel like partying. She was far too excited about what she had found out about Mr Jacobs.

'Guess what?' she asked Michaela

'What?' retorted her patient friend

'Mr Jacobs has been invited to do a talk at the Henry Pinkerton museum tonight, there was a text on his communicator about it and I've got us some tickets, we are going to go there to see him!'

'You've got to be joking!' chortled Michaela in reply 'like I want to sit with a bunch of geeks listening to boring science stuff!'

'Oh come on' responded Caitlin, 'it's my birthday and it would mean a lot to me'.

'No way Cait, you're my best friend and I don't want to see you getting hurt. Mr Jacobs isn't interested in you, get real, you're one of his students, one of many whom he doesn't even give a second's thought to', Michaela felt mean but it had to be said.

'You are so wrong' snapped Caitlin, 'he does, I know he does, I've noticed the way he looks at me'.

'Cait, he's married and you can bet his wife's a babe, you have no chance'.

Caitlin glared at her friend.

'I don't care, she's out of the picture for three months, besides she can't really love him if she's willing to be parted from him for that long. There's no way on this earth that I'd leave someone as fit as him on his own for that long!'

Michaela was speechless, Caitlin was a lost cause.

'So I'm definitely going tonight, with or without you' Caitlin hissed at her.

'Caitlin?' her mother's voice interrupted their quarrel. 'Are you in there?'.

'Yes mum' she replied. The door opened and Karel Simmons stepped in to see the two girls sitting on Caitlin's bed hunched up.

'Well, you wouldn't believe there was a big party going on today looking at you two. What's up?'

It was Michaela that answered. 'Caitlin's feeling sad that her dad won't be here, that's all'.

Karel tilted her head and looked at her daughter.

'Caitlin, we all know how you feel, we're feeling it too. However, your dad wouldn't want you to be unhappy, he'd want you to have a good time for his sake. So please, do try to lighten up a bit.' She looked for signs of improvement, but Caitlin didn't move.

'Jane's just arrived and is working wonders on Mel as we speak. After she's finished with her I thought you would like to be next is that okay?'

Caitlin looked up at her mum and managed a faint smile.

'Okay, that's fine with me' she said, it would be good to have her hair and make up done so that she would look a knock out that evening, Mr Jacobs would not be able to resist her! She kept thinking about his face when he had been trying to fix her holopod the other day, that thick dark hair contrasting so perfectly with those blue eyes, the look on his face as he battled with the technology. No, there was not a chance in hell she would ever leave him alone if he was her man!

Mel was very pleased with Jane's handiwork, she was looking good for her 116 years. She still had all her

The Present Future

faculties, could walk without the aid of a stick, thanks to the wonders of modern medicine, and her skin was as smooth as a baby's. Anti-aging technology had developed in leaps and bounds during her lifetime, and she was one of the first to benefit from the youthful longevity that went with it. She still had her natural hair colour, mid auburn, with not a grey in sight! How different things were now to when her grandmother was still alive. She sighed remembering how grandma Anna had not aged well. Her eyesight failed her, her bones were brittle and broke easily, her skin sagged and hung loosely off of her lightweight frame and latterly she lost her mobility. Thank goodness things had improved since then! Smiling at her reflection in the mirror, she turned her thoughts to what jewellery she was going to wear for the party. Her thoughts were interrupted when she saw Caitlin. She looked at her eldest great granddaughter in dismay. She looked lovely. Her long fair hair had been styled into loose curls that framed her delicately freckled face and her green eyes shone like mountain lakes. Yet she looked so sad and had hardly spoken to her that day. But Mel knew that soon the smile would be back on her face, soon she was about to embark on the biggest adventure of her life, if only she knew it!

'Cait my dear, you look like you are pining for somebody. Who is the young man?' she asked. Caitlin managed a faint smile. 'Nobody you'd know GG'

'Well whoever he is, I hope he knows how lucky he is to have somebody as lovely as you thinking about him. Why didn't you invite him to the party?'

'He wouldn't have come' replied Caitlin 'he's not into parties'.

'Never mind' said Mel soothingly 'you still have plenty

of time before you need to get serious about anybody'. She put an arm around Caitlin's shoulder.

'Things were very different when I was your age.' She sighed. 'When would it have been now, oh yes, two thousand and eleven, one hundred years ago of course! I can't believe how the time has gone' she shook her head.

'What was it like back then GG?' Caitlin asked, her mood lifting slightly.

'Well, where do I start' replied Mel. 'Things were much more basic and the world was a scary place. People were very aggressive towards each other and there were nasty terrorists planting bombs everywhere.' She had forgotten how bleak the past had been.

'Surely there must have been some good things' said Caitlin frowning.

'Of course there were' Mel smiled at her. 'Your great grandfather Sam for one. We met when we were kids, though we didn't marry until we were both thirty, we wanted to travel the world and have fun first. I can remember on my sixteenth birthday, Sam gave me a wonderful present, a silver bracelet with little pink gems inset. He had saved for ages to pay for it. I treasured it for years. In fact, I think I still have it somewhere' she paused for thought.

Caitlin looked at her in awe. She had seen videos of GG and Sam when they were young but had never actually met Sam since he died when she was still a baby. She really regretted not having known him since he looked like a fun kind of person. She was saddened to see a tear appear in GG's eye.

'I still miss him' said Mel 'all the time'. She looked Caitlin in the eye. 'I hope you find somebody as wonderful as him'.

Caitlin smiled, she already had, but he was out of her reach, for now anyway. However, soon things would be different, of that she was sure!

'I would very much like one of those cocktails they're serving' Mel said taking Caitlin by the arm. Caitlin was surprised by this.

'Isn't alcohol bad for your youth treatment?' she said

'Absolutely' replied Mel grinning.

The party was a great success and Mel was the centre of attention. She kept everybody amused with tales of her youth and endeavoured to entertain them by taking her turn on the karaoke holopod, singing along side 3D images of the old greats such as Madonna, Lady Ga Ga and Beyoncé. Karel was slightly embarrassed by all of this, but was pleased to see her grandmother enjoying herself.

Tamara was minding Gavin and the other younger children who were fighting each other with their Beetle Bots, (small robots that looked like beetles). Everything was running smoothly and everybody was having a whale of a time.

Caitlin was getting more animated as the afternoon wore on, soon she would make her escape and head over to the Henry Pinkerton museum to see her idol. She had tried to persuade Michaela to come, but Michaela was adamant that she wouldn't, so she would have to go on her own. So much for best friends! So when the clock struck 7 pm she snuck away, leaving the party still very much in progress. Mel was making her job easy for her, she had never seen her great grandmother looking so alive, nor known her to drink so many cocktails, she had everybody in raptures. As Caitlin made her escape she could have sworn that Mel winked at her, but then again, it could have been a trick of the light.

By the time she arrived at the Henry Pinkerton Museum, a crowd had already gathered outside. The talk was to take place in the garden suite, a large glass building attached to the museum that provided views of the magnificent gardens overlooking the sea during the day and the stars at night. The Henry Pinkerton Museum was situated in the grounds of the Pinkerton estate, high up on the cliff top overlooking the small regency town of Sidmouth below. The Pinkerton family no longer existed, Henry being the last in the line, had died seventy years ago leaving the house and his laboratory in trust. Everything had been preserved for posterity and the museum was constructed thirty years after his death as a means of continuing to contribute funds to the trust for the upkeep of the estate. Henry Pinkerton had been a brilliant physicist in his time, contributing much to the technological revolution, being one of the World's best inventors. It was even said that he had designed a time machine, something that he talked about a great deal with much enthusiasm. He was convinced that this machine would work, he just needed the funding to build it. However, it would seem that the funding never materialised and his dream died with him, but the legend lived on.

Caitlin looked around to see if there was anybody else there she recognised, but there wasn't. This didn't surprise her since none of her friends would have been seen dead at such an event. She followed the rest of the group into the garden suite and sat down with her complimentary glass of white wine, eagerly waiting for Mr Jacobs to appear. Looking around at the other guests she could tell that she was by far the youngest, but then again she wasn't there because she wanted to listen to some boring lecture about the human mind, she had another agenda entirely. She didn't have to wait long, minutes later the crowd was hushed by an announcement made by the compère.

'Ladies and gentlemen, I would like to extend my gratitude to you for coming tonight. As you know the Henry Pinkerton Trust relies totally on the funds generated by the museum and function rooms for its survival, so if you could all dig deep into your pockets, then it would be much appreciated'.

Oh get on with it, thought Caitlin.

'During the course of the evening we will be passing round creditometers to enable you to make contributions and there will be a raffle as well with some great prizes. In addition to this you are all invited to take a tour of the house later, a rare chance to see how the great man lived. So, without further ado, please welcome our guest speaker for tonight, here to talk about the human psyche, Mr Matthew Jacobs'.

Everybody applauded as Matt appeared.

Finally, thought Caitlin.

'Good evening folks' Matt addressed the crowd, 'before you get whisked off on a tour of this magnificent house, I'd like to take you all on a tour of a different kind, a tour of your mind', he scanned the audience as he spoke.

Caitlin stared at him in awe, he was dressed in a dark suit which showed off his well toned physique, his teeth looked extra white in the dimly lit room and his eyes seemed to have a wicked twinkle in them. She hardly listened to a word he was saying, all she could do was stare, drinking in every precious moment. She was totally oblivious to what was happening around her, so much so that she didn't hear the gasps coming from the audience, or notice that the lights had suddenly got brighter, it was only when she saw the shocked look in Mr Jacob's eyes that she realised something was afoot. She swung round to see where he was looking and saw two masked men standing in the doorway, one of them appeared to be armed.

'Okay, nobody move and nobody will get hurt' said the armed one.

The second masked man starting walking towards the front of the audience.

'Now here's what we want you to do', continued the armed man.

'First of all I want you all to throw your communicators onto the floor, then put your hands in the air, both of them. Then, my friend will be coming round to each of you with a creditometer, all you have to do is to input your bank account details into the machine and we will do the rest' he smirked. 'We'll just relieve you of a few hundred credits each, that's all, we aren't greedy!', *this was going to be easy, the combined income of these people would make him very rich indeed!* However, he hadn't reckoned on Matt Jacobs.

Matt stood silently watching as the two men set about ripping off his audience. He knew he had to do something, but he would have to be very cautious, so as not to arouse suspicion.

Caitlin suddenly felt sick and wished she hadn't been so stupid as to go there in the first place. The unarmed masked man worked his way along the room and was now level with her.

'Punch in your details sweetheart' he said holding the creditometer in front of her with a big grin on his face.

'I haven't got a bank account' she said, 'I'm only sixteen'.

The masked man looked closely at her, not knowing whether to believe her or not, *they all looked so much more grown up these days.* Caitlin stared back at him nervously fiddling with her hair. After what seemed to her like an eternity, he finally accepted her explanation and moved on. She breathed a sigh of relief and looked up to see Mr Jacobs staring right at her, looking agitated.

The masked man continued doing the rounds until everybody in the room, including Matt had provided their bank account details. Then he and his armed colleague went to make their exit, they couldn't believe how easy it had been, but as they left the garden suite things started to go pear shaped. As they emerged into the darkness something didn't seem quite right.

'Where's the path gone?' one of them asked the other. He looked around, but all he could see was the cliff edge.

'Frank?' he called out to his friend, but got no reply. He swung round 360 degrees, not able to believe his own eyes, for everywhere he looked he could see nothing but cliff edge, like he had stepped onto the edge of the world. *How in hell had that happened and where was Frank?* Frank was experiencing the same dilemma, he stood motionless, absolutely petrified, he was afraid of heights.

'Frank?' his friend called, but Frank couldn't hear him, couldn't see him, he was all alone.

A few feet behind them a man stood watching with a big grin on his face.

'Got ya' said Matt.

A short while later the police arrived, totally baffled as to what was occurring with the masked raiders. There they both were, walking round in circles, seemingly oblivious to their surroundings. They police concluded that they must have been high on drugs and whisked them away. The creditometer was retrieved and all credit returned to the bank accounts from which it was stolen and, despite the upset, many of the guests were happy to continue with their evening. After Matt concluded his talk on the human psyche, the guests were ushered away for a tour of the house and everybody tagged along, except for Matt and Caitlin.

Caitlin wasn't fussed about seeing the relics of an old fossil, she was more interested in getting some one to one time with Mr Jacobs. Matt was intrigued as to why she was there, despite his great powers of observation and his 'gift', he was totally oblivious to this girl's feelings for him, sometimes he couldn't see what was right in front of his face.

'Caitlin I didn't realise you were interested in the workings of the human mind' he said to her.

'Well actually, there's a lot you don't know about me' she replied, trying desperately not to blush.

'Oh' mused Matt, 'please enlighten me'.

'Well, for starters, we have something in common' she said, reeling him in.

Matt fixed his blue eyes on hers, making her tingle inside.

'My dad is the astronaut, Jack Simmons, and I believe your wife is a member of his crew'.

Matt was slightly taken aback by this.

'Oh really' he said, 'what a coincidence'.

'Yeah, cool don't you think?' enthused Caitlin, 'he's one of the best there is and he's very particular about

The Present Future

who crews with him, so your wife must be an exceptional woman'.

'She is' replied Matt, 'and I'm reliably informed that she couldn't wish for a better captain than your dad' he returned the compliment.

Caitlin smiled, she was on to a winner here.

'So what's it like being the daughter of one of the world's most renowned astronauts?' Matt asked.

'Difficult at times', replied Caitlin, hoping for sympathy, 'he's not around very often and I do miss him so. It was hard growing up with a dad who was rarely there for your birthday or Christmas, or other special occasions, I used to envy my friends'.

Matt's heart went out to this young woman, he knew only too well what it was like growing up without a father, his grandad had done his best, but it wasn't the same.

'Yes, I know how that feels' he said, 'my mum and dad disappeared when I was only eight and I found it hard living without them, very hard, and every time I celebrated another birthday I hoped they would return, but they never did'.

Caitlin saw a look of sadness in those blue eyes and so wanted to put her arms around him, but she knew she mustn't.

'How awful, how did they disappear?' she asked.

'They set off on a boating trip one day, an exceptionally calm day, yet despite that they never reached their intended destination and never returned. Neither the boat they were in nor their bodies were ever found, so I never got closure if you know what I mean. To this day it remains a mystery what happened on that day and I guess I'll never know now', Matt found himself momentarily lost, trying to picture their faces, yet still he could not.

'What do you think happened?' Caitlin asked, 'do you have any theories?'

'I've had many over the years, everything you can think off from being struck by a submarine to being abducted by aliens, but nothing ever gave me the answers I needed', Matt continued to stare into space, it was never easy talking about this.

Caitlin was seeing a whole new side to him, one that made her want him even more, if only she could reach out to him and............. Her thoughts were interrupted by a loud noise and the ground seemed to shake like an earthquake for a few moments.

'What was that?' she gasped.

Matt was equally surprised. The noise which sounded like a jet engine, seemed to be coming from a building in the grounds of the house, a building which had once housed Henry Pinkerton's research laboratory.

'I have absolutely no idea' said Matt, 'but I think I'll go and take a look, you had better stay here, just in case it isn't safe'.

'No way' said Caitlin in defiance, 'I'm coming with you'.

CHAPTER FIVE

Henry Pinkerton's laboratory was an imposing building set apart from the house and museum. Constructed of concrete, it was situated at the bottom end of the rambling gardens, almost hidden from view, so as not to spoil the look of the rest of the estate. A quick glance would lead you to believe that it had no windows since they were all located high up, almost at roof level, this was deliberate so that nobody could see in from ground level. Although Matt had visited the estate many times before he had never ventured inside the laboratory, it was always kept locked and was not open to the public. He was therefore surprised to see that the door appeared to be open and there was a light on inside. As he and Caitlin approached, a figure emerged from the building, stumbling as if drunk. At closer inspection they could see that it was a man of later years and he seemed to be confused.

'David is that you?' he asked, rubbing his eyes which hadn't yet focussed properly in the dark.

'No, I'm not David, my name is Matt' Matt replied.

The man looked at him warily.

'Sorry, my mistake. I don't suppose you have seen my colleague David have you?' he enquired.

'I'm afraid not' replied Matt, 'might I ask who you are?'

The man looked at him, trying to decide whether he could be trusted or not.

'I'm the owner of this establishment' he replied, 'and whose your lady friend?' he looked towards Caitlin.

'I'm Caitlin' she replied, 'are you okay, we could hear what sounded like an earthquake?'.

'I'm fine, a bit shaken, but otherwise in good shape, but thank you for asking' he smiled at her. She reminded him of one of his students.

'What was that noise we heard earlier?' asked Matt.

'Oh, that was nothing to worry about' replied the man, 'just a little experiment I've been working on'.

Matt was confused, the laboratory hadn't been used for years and the estate was no longer privately owned, belonging to the trust, so who was this man? He looked vaguely familiar. He was just about to ask when his communicator beeped indicating that he had an incoming transmission. He glanced at it to see that it was a message from Jen. Since this might be the last communication from her before the Super Vulcan began its journey into deep space, he decided to view it.

'Excuse me just one moment' he said, and turned to face the other way. He activated the hologram viewer and Jen's face appeared in front of him, she looked worried.

'Matt' she said, 'something's wrong'.

These were the words he had dreaded, his heart seemed to skip a beat on hearing them.

'We've encountered some weird kind of turbulence, the ship's instruments have gone haywire and this strange tunnel of light has appeared in front of us', Jen's eyes looked like a frightened child when she spoke. 'Matt, it seems to be pulling us towards it and the Captain can't steer us away. I'm afraid Matt, afraid it's going to swallow us up and God only knows what will happen'.

Matt watched, feeling helpless, hoping that what was about to happen wouldn't.

'Matt, I love you' Jen said, 'Matt, oh my God, NO!'. The message was terminated and Jen's image disappeared.

Matt stood silently staring at the communicator, unable to comprehend what had just happened. Caitlin and the mysterious man had also seen the transmission. Caitlin started panicking and immediately tried to contact her dad, but the signal was dead.

'What's happened Matt, what did she mean by the tunnel of light?' she asked anxiously.

'I believe I may know the answer to that' said the man.

Matt and Caitlin both looked at him.

'I'm sorry to say that I may well have caused the problem', he said, an anguished look on his face.

Matt wasn't sure he had heard him correctly.

'Excuse me, did you just say you may well have caused that to happen?'

'Indeed I did' replied the man.

'How, and, just who are you?' Matt asked.

The man sighed and beckoned for them to follow him into the laboratory.

'You'd better come inside and take a seat' he said, 'there's a lot to be explained.

Matt and Caitlin stepped into the building and were surprised to see that it was virtually empty. There were some chairs scattered about, a work top with a sink inset, a few scant cabinets and that was about it.

'Please sit down' the man gestured to them. They both complied, mesmerised by what was happening.

'Let me introduce myself' the man said, 'my name is Henry Pinkerton, Professor Henry Pinkerton'.

Matt didn't know whether to laugh or cry at the absurdity of what he had just been told.

'Henry Pinkerton died seventy years ago' he said.

The man didn't looked too pleased to hear this.

'Seventy years ago' he said, 'what year is this?'

Matt wondered whether to call somebody, yet he sensed that this man believed he was telling the truth, so he decided to play along with him for a while.

'The year is twenty one eleven' he said.

The man seemed shocked to hear this.

'My God', he said, 'I've come forward one hundred years in time'. He looked around him.

'Yet this place hasn't changed, it looks intact, well, well, well'.

Caitlin was totally dumb founded by what she was hearing, who was this odd man?

'What do you mean, you've come forward one hundred years?' she asked.

'I mean just that, I have come forward one hundred years in time' he replied.

She looked at him as if he was gone out.

'How, with a time machine?' she asked.

'Absolutely' was the terse reply, 'a time machine of sorts'.

Matt listened, interested to hear the explanation. Henry Pinkerton was purported to have invented a time machine, but the story was that it never actually worked.

'So where is it?' Caitlin asked, looking around the largely vacant room.

The man followed her gaze.

'Good point' he said, 'I suppose it didn't survive the ravages of time'.

'Then how did you get here?'

'I opened up a vortex in time' replied the man, 'back in the year two thousand and eleven'. He could see from their faces that it was going to be hard to convince them, especially as the activator which enabled him to open and shut off the vortex, appeared to have short circuited.

'Listen carefully' he said, 'while I try to explain'.

So Matt and Caitlin sat and listened to the man, both still in a state of shock over what had happened.

'I know it's hard for you to comprehend' he said, 'but I am truly Henry Pinkerton'. He paused and Matt studied his face. He certainly bore a striking resemblance to the archived pictures of Henry Pinkerton he had seen.

'When I stepped into the vortex it was two thousand and eleven, look', he said and produced a leather bound booklet. He held it right up to Matt's eyes so that he could see it clearly. Matt read the date embossed on the cover, it read 2011 but looked brand new, certainly not one hundred years old. The Professor then opened it and showed him the contents. It contained a calendar of public holidays, a mini map of the old London underground system, long since demolished and a 7 day to a page diary.

'That's very impressive, but it could be a fake' said Matt.

'Oh it's the real McCoy Matt, just like the skin on my nose' retorted the Professor.

Again Matt sensed genuine thoughts coming from the man. He was intrigued.

'How did you open this vortex in time?' he asked.

'It's complicated' replied the Professor. 'but, in a nutshell, I was working on a theory I had for many years, that if the speed at which light travels could be controlled and channelled in a precise way it could be used to warp and bend space-time'. He paused to gauge Matt and Caitlin's reaction to what he was saying before carrying on.

'So I devised a machine that would do precisely that. Using crystals, a substance called molybdenum and a series of glass prisms, I found a way of bending light beams, causing them to revolve at different speeds to each other. When the machine was activated, the extreme forces generated by the two revolving beams of light opened up a vortex, a man made worm hole through which an object could travel forwards and backwards in time in a continuous circle'.

Matt and Caitlin were enthralled by this.

'So how does the object travel through the vortex?' asked Caitlin.

'Allow me to demonstrate' said the Professor before getting up and heading for one of the cabinets in the lab. On opening the cabinet he produced a glass flask and a sheet of paper from which he tore off a sliver. He then filled the glass flask with some water from the tap over the sink and stirred the water vigorously until it was swirling like a whirlpool. Then he dropped the paper into the liquid. Matt and Caitlin watched as the sliver of paper was carried round and round by the whirlpool.

'You see, the paper represents an object being carried through time by the vortex, going round and round continuously'.

Matt was amazed, could this be true?

The professor continued to tell his tale, explaining how the time machine was developed.

'Once I had opened the vortex I realised that I would have to find some way of restricting access to it, so my colleague, David, the technical one, created a device which we called an activator that acted much like a tap, enabling us to open and shut the entrance to the vortex at will, thus ensuring it was safe and couldn't be accessed by anyone but myself or my team. The activator had a dual purpose, not only could it control access to the vortex, but it could also be set to a specific point in time, like a clock alarm, enabling us to control how far an object would travel forward in time. After this, all that remained was to try it out. So at first my team and I experimented with something small, something that could not be harmed or cause any damage. We sent a table tennis ball forward just ten minutes in time then waited ten minutes to see it materialise intact', he smiled as he spoke.

'This small act was a major breakthrough, but we needed to be sure that a living creature could travel thus without sustaining any harm, so we tried sending a lab rat forward, again ten minutes into the future. We were delighted when the rat re-appeared ten minutes later, still in one piece and totally oblivious to what it had been through', he paused to let them take in what he was saying.

'Then it was time for one of us to try. My other colleague Anthony volunteered, he felt that it was better that it wasn't myself or David, since if anything went wrong, we were the two people who had the knowledge to put it right and all would not be lost, so reluctantly I agreed and we sent him forward just ten minutes again. Then sure enough, ten minutes later he materialised in one piece. To him it had been no time at all, ten minutes flashed by in an instant. The hard bit was going to be sending an object forward and returning it to precisely the same moment in time that it left, avoiding the possibility of finding two of the same object existing at the same time which, if it were a person, could cause an anomaly. This needed careful calibration. Again we experimented first with a non human subject. We used the same lab rat but this time we attached a special device that would trigger the rat to return to exactly the same point in time that it left, so in effect it would look as though it had not been gone at all, appearing briefly ten minutes in the future, existing parallel to its future self for a short time, then disappearing in the blink of an eye. The device fitted to it would record the journey for us since the rat could not speak! I am pleased to say that it worked. The next step was for one of us to try and again Anthony volunteered. To avoid the shock of meeting his future self we agreed that after he returned from the future he would leave the room and stay away until his past self had departed. Confusing though it may sound, it was the most sensible thing to do in the circumstances. It was a tremendous risk, but one that, after careful consideration we agreed had to be taken. So Anthony bravely stepped into the vortex and travelled forward ten minutes where our future selves were able to tell him that he had succeeded as his future self had returned ten minutes ago! He then returned to the present where he was able to report that his future self would turn up right on time! So, it was after this and much celebration that we took the next big step. One of us would venture further into the future and this time, I was going to be the guinea pig. There was no way I was going to let one of my colleagues take the risk. So I took the decision to travel forward one year into the future to a specific date and time when I could be sure that my future self would make himself scarce so as not to meet me. The rest of my colleagues, all being well, would be there to witness my arrival, then I would step back into

The Present Future

the vortex and return. However, as you know something went wrong. I stepped into the vortex and emerged not one year, but one hundred years in the future and, much to my dismay, I found that the activator had closed off access to the vortex and had ceased to function, thus I find myself trapped in the future'. The Professor paused, a look of anguish came over his face.

Matt and Caitlin exchanged glances.

'Surely all is not lost' said Matt, 'if you can find a way of repairing the activator you could access the vortex from this end and return to the past, your present' Matt suggested.

'In theory yes' said the Professor, 'however, I am not a technical person. I understand the laws of physics, but not the intricate workings of computers or other devices such as the activator. It was David who designed the activator and without him, or somebody else of the same calibre, I am unable to locate the fault, or repair it'.

Caitlin came up with a suggestion.

'Why don't you let me take a look at it?' she said, 'I'm pretty good with technical things'.

The Professor considered this.

'I would imagine that the technology is probably far too primitive for you' he said.

'Well, surely it's worth a shot?' Caitlin retorted.

'Okay', agreed the Professor and he undid the activator that was attached to his wrist and handed it to her.

Caitlin studied it. She recalled seeing something like it before, it vaguely resembled the type of remote controls used for the mark 1 Beetle Bots, miniature robots, that she had loved as a child. She wondered if this David guy might have had something to do with the creation of them.

'What's David's surname?' she asked, curious.

'Starr' replied the Professor.

Of course! She had been correct in her assumption, Starr Industries had developed a whole range of gadgets including the Beetle Bots and Builder Ants, her personal favourites. This was good news, for there wasn't a single gadget produced by Starr Industries that she hadn't taken apart, adapted and put back together again at some time. She should be able to fix this activator, no problem.

There was still one thing that was unresolved and Matt was the one to address it.

'So what has all of this got to do with the disappearance of the Super Vulcan space ship that my wife was in?' he asked.

'Oh' said the Professor, 'forgive me, I had forgotten about that. I believe that when I emerged from the vortex at this end, it fluctuated causing a ripple in space and the Super Vulcan was sucked into the vortex and propelled back in time to the year 2011'.

Matt's head was spinning with all this. If what he was saying was true, then Jen was now one hundred years in the past.

'If you're right, then we have to get the vortex re-opened so that the Super Vulcan can come back' he said, 'is that possible'

'Yes' replied the Professor, 'but first I need to go back so that I can locate the Super Vulcan'.

'Then that being the case, I'm coming with you' said Matt,

'And me' chipped in Caitlin.

'No way Caitlin, it's not safe you have to stay here' Matt insisted.

The Present Future

'Absolutely not' said Caitlin, 'besides, you may need my help with the technical side of things'.

'That's assuming you can get the activator working again' said the Professor.

'Like this you mean' said Caitlin, pressing a tiny button on the side of the activator. There was a beep, then a red light flashed, followed by an almighty boom, causing the earth to shake.

Matt couldn't believe what he saw. A massive tunnel of swirling light appeared in front of them like a giant whirlpool.

'Magnificent' said the Professor 'truly magnificent, you're a genius'. He beamed at Caitlin.

'I know' she replied, modesty had never been her strong point!

'So what happens now?' asked Matt as the reality of what was happening was beginning to dawn on him.

'Come' gestured the Professor to Matt and Caitlin 'follow me'.

They both looked at the vortex nervously.

'Come on' urged the Professor, 'there's no time to waste' and he stepped into the vortex.

Matt moved towards the vortex, closely followed by Caitlin, then they both took a brave step forward into the swirling tunnel of light. Matt felt himself being drawn in slowly at first, then as he got further in he felt as if he were being sucked into a vacuum. A tremendous force pulled the three of them inwards, sweeping them off of their feet and spinning them round and round. Matt was, to his surprise, not afraid. It was like floating through a funnel of light, a strange, but oddly soporific feeling.

Looking ahead of them they could see the end, and as it got closer and closer they felt themselves falling, gently slowly, then landing with a slight bump on solid ground. They had arrived a hundred years ago.

CHAPTER SIX

PART TWO

SOMEWHERE IN SPACE ONE HUNDRED YEARS BEFORE THE LAUNCH OF THE SUPER VULCAN, IT SUDDENLY APPEARS!

Jack Simmons was well known for keeping his cool under pressure, that was part of what made him a good astronaut. The rest was down to his quick reactions and excellent piloting skills. However, at that moment in time, he was struggling to keep his composure. Since exiting the tunnel of light, things had taken a bizarre turn. Although everything looked the same, it soon became apparent that it wasn't. After losing contact with mission control, Rick, the IT specialist had tested the computers and communication systems to find out what the fault was. However, everything was in working order, no damage seemed to have been sustained by the Super Vulcan. Therefore the fault had to lie with mission control. Not wishing to risk exacerbating the problem, Jack decided to orbit the Earth, before departing into deep space. This produced even stranger findings. After orbiting the Earth three times, they discovered that all three of the space elevators had disappeared and the only other items orbiting the Earth were space junk; several old satellites and what looked like a space station, a relic from the last century. Jack was greatly puzzled by this since in all his missions he had never seen anything like it. He remembered learning about the first space station that was constructed in the twentieth century, but he had never seen it because it had been dismantled some 50 years ago after being replaced with the much larger Orbiter stations linked to the space elevators. There was something very wrong.

'What's the plan Jack?' asked Bob his number two.

Jack scanned his instruments, trying to hide his concern. 'Well Bob I think in the circumstances we will have to abort the deep space mission and return to Earth'.

'I was thinking the same' said Bob. 'However, we seem to have lost the Orbiters, do you think what we went through was some kind of wormhole?'

'I would, but for the fact that we are still in our own solar system, or at least one that is identical to it' replied Jack.

'Perhaps this is an alternative universe' said Bob.

Jack had never been one to believe in alternative universes, but following their trip through the tunnel of light he was beginning to lean towards the possibility. How could all three Orbiters have just disappeared like that? Common sense dictated that they couldn't, yet they were nowhere to be seen. There was only one thing for it, they would have to return to Earth using the fusion propulsion engines, they had enough fuel to do it.

'We're going to return to Earth' he said to Bob 'and since the elevators seem to have disappeared, we will have to carry out an engine assisted re-entry and landing, so tell everybody to get prepared'.

'Roger Captain, what shall I tell them?', Bob asked.

'Tell them that due to unexpected problems following the turbulence we experienced we are going to have to abort the mission for now and return to Earth by the quickest means. I don't want them to know about the missing Orbiters yet'.

'Copy that' replied Bob.

Jen Jacobs fiddled with the communicator on her wrist. It was mounted on a bracelet made of Pearlite, a metal discovered on Mars that had a pearl like texture. It had been a birthday present from Matt last year and was her most precious possession. She pressed the digitex display and watched a video from their holiday in the Italian lakes last summer. She had over a 100 videos stored on the communicator and had watched many of them since their departure. Now that she was unable to communicate with Matt, the videos were of great comfort to her. She had no idea what was happening in the control deck. All she knew was that they had lost all communications with the outside world after experiencing the weird turbulence and being sucked into the strange tunnel of light. The adventure she had so looked forward to, was fast turning into a nightmare. It wasn't as if she hadn't considered the possibility that something might go wrong, but if she was honest to herself, she didn't really believe that it would. Now there was a very real prospect that she might never see Matt again and that was something she hadn't prepared for. Her thoughts were interrupted by a knock on the door of her cabin.

'Come in' she called out.

The automatic door slid open to reveal Bob Gilmore.

'Hi Jen, how are you doing?' he asked, trying to sound as if everything was normal.

'I'm great thank you Bob, how about you?'

'Surviving' was his terse reply.

'Listen Jen, there's something you need to know' the tone of his voice changed to a serious one.

Jen felt a tinge of nerves, was this something she really wanted to hear?

'You are no doubt aware that things haven't exactly been going to plan' Bob continued.

'I had noticed' Jen replied.

'Well, the Captain has decided to abort the deep space mission and return to Earth.'

Jen wasn't surprised by this.

'However, due to the fact that we experienced a few problems following the turbulence, nothing serious I must add, we are going to do a re-entry and landing sequence, as opposed to docking to an Orbiter'.

Jen gasped, she certainly hadn't expected that.

'It's nothing to worry about Jen, it will be just like you practiced in training. In fact, you are privileged to be able to go through a re-entry and landing like this, very few have experienced it'. Bob tried to calm her nerves.

'Okay' said Jen, 'when will this take place?'.

'I don't know the exact time, but everybody needs to convene at the control deck at 12 hundred hours' Bob replied.

'Okay' said Jen, consulting her communicator 'that's two hours from now'.

'See you then' grinned Bob before backing out of the cabin.

'See you' said Jen, trying to hide the fact that she was terrified. It was true that they had gone through a re-entry sequence in training, but that was assuming everything was in working order. What if there was a malfunction, what then? She shuddered at the thought.

The rest of the crew were similarly unsettled, but like

The Present Future

Jen, hid their concern. Aside from Jack, Bob and Rick, there were four other crew members. Jen was the only first timer, the others were Sue, an aeronautical engineer, Pete a botanist and Wayne a Medic. They had all done space travel before, however, in common with Jen, none of them had experienced a re-entry and landing, this was a first for everyone.

Jack read the check list for a re-entry in the Super Vulcan over and over again. Even though the computer would carry out the procedure he didn't want to have to rely on that alone. He only hoped that the Super Vulcan hadn't sustained any undetected damage to her structure and that she could cope with the stresses that would be placed on her during the re-entry. The other concern was the fusion propulsion engines, would they work? Without them, they wouldn't be able to enter the Earth's atmosphere and would be stranded in space for ever. Albeit they had been tested prior to launch, they had not been engaged since. He wasn't worried about the flight and landing, once they were back in the Earth's atmosphere, that would be just plain sailing for him. Even should the engines fail at that point, he was confident he could glide the thing down.

At that moment the communication module came to life. He turned to Rick.

'Rick, what's occurring?'.

Rick looked at his instruments, a puzzled expression on his face.

'I can't explain it' he said. 'I'm getting signals from Earth, but not on any of the usual frequencies' he said.

'For some strange reason they appear to be using an S-band frequency, one that hasn't been used for over 50 years'.

'Can we pick it up?' asked Jack.

'I'm trying' replied Rick, his fingers furiously tapping the controls. 'Aaah' he said 'I think I have it. I'll patch it through to the main speakers'.

The speakers on the control deck popped, then a voice came over loud and clear.

'Unknown spacecraft, this is Mission Control, Houston, please identify yourself'. The message was repeated several times, both in English and what appeared to be Russian.

'Can we respond?' asked Jack.

'Indeed we can Captain. I'll open a communication channel for you'.

Flight Director Frank Hudson was on the phone to the Administrator, who in turn was on the hotline to the President. The air at the Johnson Space Centre had been electric, ever since the unknown spacecraft had been picked up by satellite and images relayed back to Earth. The Orbiter Space Station had also reported seeing it go past at least three times. At first they had thought it to be an alien visitation, but the images had revealed that its origins had to have been that of Earth. The giant vessel was like nothing they had seen before, but could only dream of developing in the future. The tell tale signs that it was of their world were the markings on it. On both the port and starboard sides they had seen the letters S-VULCAN 2111. They had spent many hours conversing with their Russian counterparts who had assured them that it wasn't theirs, and an equal amount of time assuring the Russians that it wasn't a US craft. Then, between them they had argued as to which other nation might have the technology and money to develop such a machine. Could

The Present Future

it be the Japanese, Koreans or Arabs? These were the most likely. However, the markings suggested otherwise. The word VULCAN brought to mind the old British bomber plane, and indeed, it did bear a resemblance to it, but how could the British keep something like that a secret? It was highly unlikely that they would. A few more phone calls led to a few more denials and everybody was completed perplexed as to whom it belonged. Certainly nobody was ready to admit it was theirs. The solution to finding out was to try and communicate with it somehow. This was down to Frank Hudson, today, was a day he would never forget.

'Sir, we are getting a signal from the unknown craft' said Jimmy one of his controllers.

Frank leaped over to his console and listened in. The message came over loud and clear.

'Mission Control, this is Super Vulcan twenty one eleven, do you read me?'.

Frank was stunned.

'Roger Super Vulcan twenty one eleven, please state the Captain's name and point of departure'. Frank couldn't believe he was communicating with the craft as if it were perfectly normal.

The message was being broadcast over loudspeakers in the control room and all staff were fixated.

'Roger, the Captain's name is Jack Simmons and the departure point was Orbiter three, on August 19 twenty one eleven'.

Frank, turned to Jimmy to seek clarification, since he didn't believe his own ears.

'Jimmy did he just say twenty one eleven or did I mishear, was it twenty eleven?'. Jimmy looked equally baffled.

'It was twenty one eleven sir' he confirmed.

Frank raised his eyebrows in surprise. It had to be a hoax, it couldn't be for real.

'Super Vulcan twenty one eleven, please confirm the location of Orbiter three' he found himself requesting.

There was a delay before the response came through as if the person speaking was surprised by the question.

'Orbiter three is located on Space Elevator three at grid reference 51°29'10.75м North, 0°08'14.09м West, 22,000 miles above the Earth in geostationary orbit'.

Frank didn't know how to respond to this. Could he be dreaming, or was this really happening? Was it possible that this spacecraft had somehow travelled back in time from a hundred years in the future? It would certainly explain the superior design and technology they were witnessing. He decided to address the Captain again.

'Super Vulcan' he said, dropping the twenty one eleven.

'Please confirm your intention'.

The response he got, was most welcome.

'Mission Control, our intention is to perform a re-entry and landing. We estimate re-entry at thirteen hundred hours at which point we should be positioned in an orbit with a 57 degree inclination to the equator. Please confirm any traffic in the area.'

Frank was taken aback. In all his twenty years at NASA he had never imagined he would see a day like today.

He had made the decision not to shock the crew of the Super Vulcan by telling them that they were arriving one hundred years in the past. He didn't want them to abort. The Administrator and President would not thank him for letting this go. Instead he chose to acknowledge their request and sound as normal as possible.

'Roger Super Vulcan, no other traffic anticipated we will monitor your descent from 145,000 feet, please confirm your intended point of landing .'

'Eurobase' was the reply.

Eurobase, where the hell is that?, thought Frank, he was going to ask for clarification but then thought better of it, not wanting to rock the boat. Once they had picked up the unknown vessel on radar they could track its route and pinpoint where it had landed.

The course was set. Today they were going to make history!

The crew were all strapped in and ready for re-entry. They all engaged in small talk in an effort to alleviate their nerves. Jen admired Sue, an aeronautical engineer and seasoned space traveller, what an enviable profession. More and more females were moving into the space industry and Jen had a hankering to join them, she had always wanted to be a space scientist and travel the universe. Despite the fact that she was at the moment in time terrified of her predicament, at the same time she confessed to feeling a tinge of excitement. The rest of the crew were just plain terrified!

'Okay crew' Jack addressed them. 'Prepare yourselves for re-entry'.

The time had come to return to Earth.

Jack initiated the re-entry programme on the computer and waited for the sequence to commence. The friendly female voice of the computer relayed each stage of the procedure as it happened.

'Fusion propulsion primers selected'

'Confirm green lights indicating engines fully primed'

'Confirm outlet valves opened'

'Confirm temperature and pressure within normal operating range'

'Ignition activated'

Bob turned to Jack and smiled.

They both waited patiently for the engines to respond. At first there was nothing and it seemed like the engines weren't going to ignite. Jack felt his heartbeat increase 'don't fail me now' he thought. Without the propulsion engines there was no way of blasting their way into the Earth's atmosphere.

'Come on baby' he said out loud.

Almost as if by command the Super Vulcan's engines burst into life and both pilots breathed a sigh of relief.

'Ignition successful, positioning for re-entry' the computer confirmed.

The gauges indicated that everything was in working order. They were ready for their descent.

Shortly after 1300 hours the Super Vulcan entered the Earth's atmosphere at an altitude of about 400,000 feet. At this point its kinetic converters kicked in, producing enough energy to power the cooling systems for the engines and leading edge surfaces, preventing overheating due to the sheer velocity of the descent.

This was the most critical point of the re-entry. If the kinetic converters failed, the Super Vulcan could overheat and disintegrate.

Jack took his mind off of this possibility by thinking ahead to the approach and landing.

At mission control, Frank Hudson and his team waited eagerly for the next transmission.

The Present Future

Jen Jacobs was mesmerized as she looked out of the portholes from the control deck. The initial fear she had felt when they commenced the re-entry was soon replaced with a feeling of wonderment as she saw the magical aurora of the plasma created by the de-orbit burn, it was better than any firework display she had ever seen. There was no horrible feeling of acceleration, which is what she had most feared, instead it felt like they were drifting down through a beautiful blue lagoon – it was surreal.

Jack Simmons began to relax as he realised the Super Vulcan wasn't going to break up and concentrated on the task ahead of him. He continued the descent towards Eurobase. The sonic boom was heard across parts of Europe, but nobody batted an eyelid, assuming it to be a military jet. Any sightings of the Super Vulcan wouldn't have caused much excitement to the average person, since it looked just like any other military jet from that distance.

In slightly less than 30 minutes the Super Vulcan was positioned above where the Eurobase should be, only it wasn't. Jack was no longer surprised by this, he was now coming to terms with the fact that they had somehow strayed into some unknown territory, it was Earth, but not the Earth they knew. He touched down with perfect precision on the big empty land mass that was later to become the first European space station.

'I don't understand, where's Eurobase?' a confused Bob Gilmore asked his captain.

'I've no idea Bob' replied Jack, equally confused, 'but I intend to get to the bottom of this'.

The two of them stared at the vast expanse of wasteland that surrounded them.

'Let's get out and take a look' said Jack. He unstrapped

himself and stood up, his legs were a bit shaky after the descent.

'What should we tell the crew?' asked Rick who had remained silent after losing radio contact with mission control (though not the mission control he was used to speaking to!).

Jack thought about that for a moment before answering succinctly,

'The truth'.

The three of them went into the main seating area where the rest of the crew were still strapped in, discussing what had happened.

'How are you all doing?' asked Jack.

Everybody looked up at him, they were mostly grateful to be alive.

'We're fine' replied Jen on their behalf, 'but I suppose we all want to know what happened back there, what was that tunnel of light, was it a worm hole?'

Jack looked at Jen. She was the rookie, the scientist who had never ventured into space before. He had seen her CV and test results from the space training and had been impressed.

'To be honest, we don't know' replied Jack, 'there is a possibility that we went through some kind of a worm hole, certainly the Earth is not the same as it was when we set off, but we can't be sure for now'.

'So what's the plan, have you managed to contact anybody for help?' Jen asked.

'We did make contact with mission control during our descent, but since then we've heard nothing, all our radio equipment seems to have malfunctioned'. Bob replied.

Jen looked concerned, she had tried using her

communicator, but that too seemed dead. The rest of the crew had the same problem.

'Bob and myself will go outside and take a look around. In the meantime I want the rest of you to stay here until we get back. Keep the exits sealed, do you understand?' Jack asked them all.

'Roger captain' they all replied. However, Jen wasn't having any of it, she intended to go with them.

'Okay, we won't be long I promise' Jack tried to reassure them. He then turned to Bob, 'happy with that Bob?' he asked. Bob nodded in response, then the two of them went to the disembarkment area, followed by Jen.

Bob touched a screen on the wall which was almost hidden by photos of the crew and, as if by magic, a door shaped opening appeared in the fuselage of the Super Vulcan. Moments later some steps sprang out and rolled all the way to the ground. Jen was impressed, having joined the Super Vulcan in space, she hadn't witnessed this before.

Jack started to descend followed by Bob and Jen.

The three of them stepped out into the fresh air and breathed it in as if it were an intoxicating drug.

'Well, that's good to know' said Bob, 'the air is breathable at least!'

'Hey, Jen, I thought I told you to stay on board!' Jack said, suddenly noticing her presence.

'Sorry captain' Jen apologised, 'but I couldn't help myself' she shrugged. Jack couldn't help but smile to himself.

'I'll let you off this time' he said to her sternly, 'but next time you disobey an order I'll have to reprimand you, understand?'.

'Yes captain' she replied, trying not to blush with embarrassment.

Jack looked into the pixie like face with the big brown eyes, somehow he knew she was nobody's fool!

'Welcome to the team' he said grinning.

Before any of them was able to say another word, they heard the sound of approaching vehicles. They looked over to where the noise was coming from and saw two military style trucks.

'Oh my god' said Bob, 'this must be some kind of a pageant!'. The last time he saw trucks like that was when he went to the transport museum as a child. The three of them watched as the trucks drew nearer to them, leaving a trail of dust in their wake. They were too stunned to move. The trucks pulled up right in front of them and stopped. Then the doors opened and several men dressed in kaki uniforms got out. Jack couldn't help but notice they were carrying guns.

'Put your hands up and don't move' one of the soldiers shouted.

Jack looked at Bob and Jen. 'Better do as they say' he instructed them. So the three of them raised their hands above their heads.

'Excellent' said a bald headed man, who suddenly appeared form behind the soldiers. He wasn't wearing a uniform, but was dressed in a black suit, making him look official. He was a small man with a face like a weasel.

'Who the hell are you?' asked Bob.

'Peter Harper' replied the man, 'your new commander'.

Bob looked at Jack and shrugged his shoulders.

'Would you care to explain?' Jack addressed Harper.

'All in good time' was the reply, 'but first we have to

The Present Future

get you and this magnificent creature to a more secure location'. He looked at the Super Vulcan in amazement, he had never seen anything quite like it before. The solar panels glistened in the sunlight making it look like a giant diamond. He wondered just how much more advanced technology could get. If Anthony had been correct, then he was looking at the future of space travel, one hundred years in the future to be precise! He was going to be so powerful with this knowledge in his possession!

'We're not going anywhere until you show us some ID' interrupted Jack.

Harper tutted at him.

'I'm afraid you have no choice' he gestured to the soldiers who raised their guns.

'Now, take us on board, captain, am I right in assuming that you are the captain of this vessel?'

Jack frowned at the weasel, 'absolutely' he replied, 'and as such I have the safety of my crew to consider'.

Harper laughed and grabbed Jen by the arm, pulling her towards him.

'Ouch, let go of me shorty' she hissed at him.

Harper was not impressed, he had a complex about his height.

'Oh you are a pretty thing' he said, 'I'd hate to see you get hurt', he ran a finger down the back of her spine, making her shudder.

'Now, take us on board or the lady loses her looks' he said to Jack, before producing a knife and holding it against Jen's face. Jack glared at Harper, *nobody threatened his crew and got away with it!*

'Alright, you've made your point' he grunted, 'Bob lead the way, I'll make sure Jen is okay'.

'That's better' said Harper, putting the knife back in

his pocket, 'bring the sonic silencer' he ordered one of the soldiers.

'Right away Sir' the soldier replied and proceeded to open the back of one of the trucks. He leant inside and lifted out a large black box.

'What's that?' asked Jack.

'Some insurance' relied Harper.

Harper and two of the soldiers, including the one with the black box, followed Jack, Bob and Jen into the Super Vulcan. Harper was even more mesmerised by the interior than he had been by the exterior.

'Ordinarily I'd ask for a guided tour, but that will have to wait' he said to Jack, 'now we need to get moving, take me to the cockpit' he demanded.

'You' he addressed one of the soldiers, 'take the lovely lady and find the rest of the crew. Make sure they are kept under control'.

'Yes Sir' replied the soldier, gesturing to Jen to show him the way. Reluctantly she took him to where the rest of the crew were waiting. Bob and Jack were coerced into taking Harper and the soldier with the black box to the cockpit.

Harper was impressed by the array of controls. Rick, the IT expert, who hadn't left the cockpit since they landed was startled by the sudden appearance of these strangers.

'What the hell' he said.

'It's okay' said Jack, 'just do as the man says'.

Harper smiled at him, 'now we are beginning to make progress' he said. He turned to the soldier with the black box.

'Activate the sonic silencer' he said.

'Yes Sir' replied the soldier before opening the black

box to reveal a control panel. After pressing a few buttons, the black box came to life and started emitting a pulsing sound.

'Are we now invisible?' asked Harper.

'Affirmative' replied the soldier.

'Excellent' said Harper, 'now let's get this bird airborne' he turned to Jack.

'Captain' he addressed him, 'I want you to take us to this location' he produced a piece of paper with some co-ordinates on which he hoped would make sense to the man from the future. Luckily for him, Jack Simmons didn't rely entirely on satellite navigation techniques! So, it was with a heavy heart that he started up the Super Vulcan's engines, which hardly seemed to have been affected by the unplanned re-entry and descent to Earth, and followed the course plotted by the irritating man to an unknown location. He only hoped that they could get out of this mess!

The Super Vulcan arrived at the mystery location, which Jack managed to glean was somewhere in the South West of England, close to his home! The Super Vulcan was set down and guided into a large hangar where it would be hidden from view. The crew were all made to disembark and were taken into what transpired to be a quarantine bay. They were each instructed to strip off and take a shower, following which they were issued with new clothing and placed into a holding area, where the door was firmly locked behind them.

'Why are you doing this to us?' Jen asked a lady who was dressed in a forensic suit with a mask protecting her face.

'We need to make sure you haven't been exposed to

anything radioactive out there' was the reply, 'don't worry you'll soon be able to go home'.

'A likely story' Jen said under her breath. There was something very wrong and she suspected that they were all in great danger.

'Matt, where are you?' she found herself asking out loud, 'please come find me'. For one brief moment she could have sworn she heard him saying 'don't worry Jen, I will', but she guessed it was just her imagination.

Peter Harper looked at his reflection in the mirror of his wash room.

'You are a genius' he said to himself, 'all you need is the device which opens the vortex in time and you will be the master of destiny!'. He ran some water into the wash basin and splashed his face, he needed to keep cool. After drying himself off he went into the command room where two other men were waiting. One of them was Anthony Stone and the other a pony tailed man, who, for some strange reason known only to himself, preferred to remain anonymous.

'Have you found David Starr yet?' Harper asked them.

'No, we're working on it' replied Stone, 'it's only a matter of time'.

'What are you standing there for then!' shouted Harper, 'Go get him!'. Why had he employed such imbeciles?

CHAPTER SEVEN

Professor Pinkerton looked worried, things weren't as they should be. The laboratory looked deserted, where were David and Anthony? They should be here exactly where they were when he departed. He looked around him to see what else was out of place.

'Oh dear' he said

'What, what's wrong?' asked Matt

The Professor pointed towards a large clock on the far corner which had a digital date display. It appeared they had arrived later than planned. It was 19 September 2011, ten days later.

Matt was not happy to see this.

'Can we go back into the vortex to the right date?' he asked.

The Professor sighed.

'Well the truth is Matt, despite my calibrations this is a new invention, and not as accurate as I would have hoped. It worked before with David and the lab rat, but then they only went forward ten minutes and I was only supposed to go forward one year. So we could go back but there are no guarantees and to do so might upset the time space continuum if we got it wrong and went back too far'.

Matt's anxiety was growing, if the activator wasn't that accurate, how could they be sure that Jen was even in that time?

'Great' he said, 'so how do we know if and when the Super Vulcan arrived?'

'Well' said the Professor, 'we'll have to check the internet, something like that is bound to have been spotted and made the news.'

'What about the rest of your team, where are they?' asked Caitlin

'I don't know, but I intend to find out' replied the Professor, 'they should be able to explain what happened at this end. Come, let's go to my office in the house' he gestured for them to follow and they emerged from the dark laboratory into bright sunlight. The house and grounds looked just the same as in the future apart from the absence of the museum and garden suite which hadn't been built yet. They made their way up to the house which had stunning views to the sea below. Matt and Caitlin found it strange to be so near to home, yet so far away. Looking around at their surroundings, they could have been anywhere in time. For a moment Matt was devoid of all feeling, detached from reality. Then suddenly he became aware of the fact that they were one hundred years in the past. He knew exactly what was going to happen over the next hundred years, so much so that he could almost defy fate. He was painfully aware, however, that Jen and the crew of the Super Vulcan were out there somewhere and anything could happen to them. He only hoped they could find them before it was too late.

As if reading his thoughts the Professor said 'don't worry Matt, we'll find your wife. I'm sure my team will be able to help'.

'Well, I wish I shared your confidence' responded Matt, 'however, right now your team don't appear to be here and we don't know exactly when the Super Vulcan came out of the vortex'.

Matt felt sure that there was something awry with the

The Present Future

Professor's team, something that would explain why he had really been stranded in the future. Perhaps somebody in his team, had their own hidden agenda?

The Professor's house appeared to be empty, nobody was home. Not even the Professor's housekeeper Margaret was present, nor had she left a note to explain where she had gone. Which was strange since Margaret, being used to the Professor disappearing for hours on end in his laboratory, always left him a note when she went out. Things were clearly not as they should be. The house itself was immaculate. Tastefully furnished with antiques from the nineteenth century, it could easily have passed for a stately home. There were portraits on the walls and everything smelt of polish. Save for the ticking of the grandfather clock in the hall, it was silent. The Professor led them to his study where he kept his laptop computer which looked like something out of the Ark to Matt and Caitlin. The Professor powered up the computer hoping that it might yield some clues. He also checked his answer phone for messages, but there were none. No e-mails, no messages, nothing to indicate what had happened in his absence. The whole thing was very disturbing.

However, the internet yielded some good news, the Super Vulcan had arrived, there were countless pictures of it captured by curious people all over Europe on their mobile phones and digital cameras. It was variously described as a new stealth bomber, prototype space shuttle or military jet built using alien technology. Enthusiasts claimed to have picked up a radio transmission between mission control and some unidentified space craft which claimed to have departed from a space station one hundred years in the future, though NASA denied this, claiming it was a hoax. They also denied that it was a prototype of a new space shuttle. Whoever designed and built the Super Vulcan had not come forward and nobody was able to verify its whereabouts since its arrival ten days ago, it seemed to have disappeared. There were many rumours as to its fate, the most popular being that it was being housed in a giant hangar somewhere in Europe, some even said that it was like the Roswell incident all over again. One thing was for sure, whoever knew the answers was keeping very quiet about it.

The Professor turned to Matt and Caitlin who were both disturbed by what they saw.

'How do we even begin to find out where it is?' said Caitlin in despair.

'I have a friend who works for the Kennedy Space Programme who may be able to help' said the Professor, 'I'll give him a call'. On that note he picked up the phone, selected the number from the address book, pressed okay, and waited for the call to connect. The phone rang several times before it was answered, the Professor put it onto speaker phone so they could all hear the person on the other end.

'Frank Hudson' the voice said.

'Hi Frank, it's Henry Pinkerton, how are you doing?' the Professor asked.

'Well hi Henry, I'm fine, long time no speak, how are you?' replied Frank.

'Not bad for an old geezer of sixty, who has no plans to retire yet' quipped the Professor.

Frank laughed, 'there's plenty of life in the old dog yet, so what can I do for you Henry?'

'Well I was hoping you could help to solve a mystery that has been the subject of much discussion at the University here for the last week' the Professor said.

'Oh, what might that be?' asked Frank.

'What's the story on the Super Vulcan, I believe its called, is it one of yours, do you know where it is?'

Frank laughed again, 'oh Henry don't I wish!' he said, 'the truth is nobody knows, or at least is admitting to know its origins or current whereabouts. All I can tell you is that it isn't anything to do with us. I won't lie to you Henry because you're a pal and we go back many years, but I know very little about the Super Vulcan, other than it was picked up 10 days ago orbiting the Earth. We managed to make contact with it and tracked its entry into the Earth's atmosphere and the route it took before it landed. After that it just disappeared, we weren't able to re-establish contact with it and it's not been seen or heard of since.'

'Are you able to confirm where it landed?' the Professor asked.

'Certainly' said Frank, 'it was in England, rather coincidently your neck of the woods, however, if you're planning to send your own search party I can save you a lot of time because our contacts in London searched the whole area for miles and found nothing'.

'I'd still like to know' said the Professor.

'Very well' said Frank and he gave the Professor the map reference of the spot where the Super Vulcan had landed.

'Many thanks Frank, give my regards to your family' said the Professor.

'You're welcome' replied Frank, 'but as you know, this conversation never took place!'

'Absolutely' replied the Professor and they both said goodbye before terminating the call.

The Professor was about to say something to Matt

when a pinging sound came from his computer, then an instant message appeared on the screen. It said 'video call requested with Anthony Stone – accept/decline'. The Professor was relieved to see this, he turned to Matt and said 'here could be the answer we need as to what happened at this end after I entered the vortex'.

He adjusted the webcam so that only his face could be seen.

'I think it wise to keep the two of you out of view for the present' he said.

'Agreed' said Matt, 'we have to be careful who we trust until we get to the truth' he looked at Caitlin, poor kid, how must she be feeling? Caitlin seemed mesmerized and fascinated by the antiquated computer.

The Professor selected 'accept' and Anthony Stone's face appeared on the screen. He was much younger than the Professor, from the look of him somewhere in his mid thirties, with thin sandy coloured hair and square framed glasses.

'Henry' he said 'is that really you?'

'Of course' replied the Professor 'you are obviously surprised to see me Anthony. Would you like to explain what the hell is going on'.

Anthony Stone's face was full of concern.

'I knew you'd make it back somehow Henry. I knew it was only a matter of time. I'm so glad to see you'.

'I'm glad to see you too Anthony, but will be even more glad once you tell me why you left me stranded'.

'I fully intend to Henry, but for security reasons I can't do it over the net. All I can say is that things happened that weren't under our control, things we couldn't possibly have anticipated.' He hesitated looking nervously over his shoulder at something.

The Present Future

'What are you talking about Anthony, what things and where the hell are you?' the Professor was concerned.

Anthony Stone looked increasingly anxious, as if he were expecting something nasty to happen.

'Like I said Henry, we can't talk here. It would be safer if we met up somewhere where we can't be overheard'.

The Professor found Stone's attitude both irritating and disturbing. Nevertheless he needed to get to the bottom of this.

'Okay Anthony, where do you suggest?'.

'Your favourite view point at Woodbury Common an hour from now'.

'Okay' replied the Professor 'will David be with you?'

'No' replied Stone 'David………' before he could finish what he was about to say his image was replaced with a text window with the words 'video call terminated' and he was gone. Despite several attempts, the Professor was unable to make contact with him again.

'What happened?' asked Matt.

'The connection is lost' replied the Professor 'I can't seem to get it back, I have no other choice than to go and meet him'.

'What about the Super Vulcan?' asked Caitlin, 'surely our priority is to try and find it?'

'Agreed' said Matt, 'Professor, where was the location where it landed?'

'Approximately 25 miles south of here' the Professor replied, 'however, as Frank said, his team carried out a thorough search of the area and found nothing, so we would be going on a wild goose chase if we were to head over there right now. Might I suggest that we find out what Anthony has to say before we do anything else, it's just possible he may know something'.

Caitlin didn't look happy, she needed to know her dad was alright.

'We are wasting valuable time, why don't we try using our communicators to see if we can get hold of them?' she suggested to Matt.

'Good point' replied Matt, 'however, I doubt they will work in this era', he activated his communicator, but as he suspected, there was no signal available. Caitlin had the same problem.

'Great' he said, 'we're not doing very well here, the Super Vulcan has disappeared once again and we have no way of communicating with its crew or locating it'. He had a sudden thought. 'Professor, is it possible that your team might have discovered the anomaly and sent the Super Vulcan somewhere else in time in an effort to return it?'

The Professor considered this.

'It's possible, which is why I think I should meet up with Anthony, he may have the answers'.

'Well, that being the case I think I should come with you' said Matt. He checked the time on the clock in the Professor's study.

'I suggest we get there early and I will remain out of sight when you meet with Anthony, just in case there are any problems'.

'Okay' replied the Professor 'as it happens Woodbury Common lends itself to plenty of hiding places with many pine trees and brambles to choose from'.

'I know' replied Matt, 'but as it happens, I don't have to rely on trees'.

The Professor looked puzzled by this answer until

Matt gave him a demonstration by way of explanation. For, much to his surprise, right in front of his eyes Matt suddenly disappeared.

'Matt?' he asked looking around him, 'where are you?'.

'I'm right here' replied Matt, re-appearing again 'I've not been anywhere'.

The Professor was completely taken aback and so was Caitlin who had also witnessed the temporary disappearance.

'How on earth did you manage that?' he asked.

'It's all to do with the power of suggestion' replied Matt 'I haven't got time to explain fully, but let's just say that I was born with the ability to influence the way people see and experience things'.

Both Caitlin and the Professor were stunned. Neither had ever seen anything like it before, not in the flesh anyway.

'It's not something I'm proud of' said Matt 'in fact, I've suppressed it for many years not wishing to become a freak show. However, I always knew that it would come in handy one day'.

Caitlin found herself blushing.

'Can you read minds as well?' she asked.

Matt smiled at her 'yes, but it's not something I do as a rule. I respect a person's right to privacy'.

Caitlin hoped that he hadn't read her mind. She remembered a conversation she had had with Michaela, where Michaela was convinced that Mr. Jacobs could read her thoughts. How eerie that it had turned out to be true! What would Michaela think if she knew? Caitlin felt a lump in her throat at the thought of her best friend. Right now she wished Michaela was with her, but she wasn't,

Caroline Hunter

she hadn't even been born yet! She couldn't quite get her head round the fact that she was in the past, one hundred years away from the life she knew. Michaela had no idea where she was and she hadn't told anybody about her plan to follow Mr. Jacobs that day - what if she couldn't get back?

She felt Matt's eyes on her and tried to clear her mind of all thoughts just in case.

'It's okay Caitlin' he said 'I promise I won't read your mind'.

'Well I sincerely hope not' she replied indignantly.

The Professor interrupted.

'I think we had better make tracks' he said, 'hopefully my car has plenty of petrol in it', he was unable to recall when he last filled it up.

Matt had forgotten that he was in an era when vehicles were still powered by fossil fuels and were driven on tarmac roads. It would be an interesting experience indeed.

'Right, where do you keep it?' he asked.

'In the garage' the Professor replied 'now where did I leave the keys?'. He wandered off looking for them.

Matt turned to Caitlin.

'Caitlin, I think it would be safer for you to wait here until we get back'.

Caitlin was not pleased with this suggestion. She had no desire to be on her own in this strange place.

'Why can't I come too?' she asked.

'Because we don't know what to expect' he replied. 'If anything should happen when we are gone, if the Professor's housekeeper or anybody else turns up, try to make yourself scarce. If not, then make something up as to who you are.'

'Like what?' she asked.

'Come on Caitlin, I know you better than that. You're a very clever girl, tell them that you are a friend of the family or something'.

Caitlin was not amused. She had no intention of staying in that house. If she couldn't go with them, then she would have to find her own way out of there.

'Look' Matt interrupted her thoughts, 'we won't be long, have a look around, I'm sure the Professor won't mind will you Professor?' Matt called out to the Professor who had discovered his car keys.

The Professor walked over to them and looked at Caitlin sympathetically. 'Not at all, help yourself to anything you need. It's unlikely that you will have any visitors. I don't get visitors very often on account of the fact that I spend most of my time locked away in the laboratory. The only person likely to turn up is Margaret my housekeeper and you have nothing to worry about with her. Just tell her that you are the daughter of a colleague of mine and that we have gone out for a while'.

Caitlin decided that she would be better off playing along with them, at least until they had gone.

'Okay, point taken' she said.

On that note, Matt and the Professor started to make their way to the garage where they were pleased to see that a dark green Rover was waiting for them.

CHAPTER EIGHT

Caitlin waited until they had driven off before making her bid for freedom. She had no idea how long they would be, or if they would ever return. One thing was for certain, she wasn't going to wait to find out. She would go and explore for herself. She left them a note saying that she had gone for a walk in case they got back before she did.

She followed the drive from the house to the road, then took the coast path down to the town of Sidmouth below. It was a warm afternoon and nobody gave Caitlin a second glance as she walked past them. Really people in general didn't look that different and neither she supposed did she. Over the years fashions changed, new materials were developed, but there were limits to the number of designs and colours. She looked pretty much like a sixteen year old girl would have done in 2011. Her hair was long and in no particular style, she wore a pair of Lyntex trousers, but nobody would have guessed they weren't made of cotton unless they saw them get wet. Lyntex was a material which dried in less than a minute and it didn't rip, so was very practical. The top she was wearing was also made of Lyntex and had a V neck and short sleeves. Both trousers and top were a pale pink colour and went perfectly with her white ankle boots. They were made of leather, a material that was still very much in vogue in 2111. The only thing she didn't have was money. Cash was something that had long since gone out of production. In 2111 you didn't even need debit or credit cards, payment was taken straight from your account using creditometers and a machine that read your retina to ensure that you were who you said you were. She only hoped that she could get by without hard cash on that occasion.

As she strolled down the path to the town, she was pleased to see that it all looked pretty much the same as in her time. There were a few noticeable differences, the cars for one and some of the hotels and cafes no longer existed in her time. Caitlin felt suddenly honoured to be able to see things as they used to be. She admired the pretty painted buildings that faced the sea and longed to look inside them. To see things with the same eyes that her Great Gran had once done.

'GG Mel' she suddenly said out loud to herself. Of course, GG Mel was alive in 2011, what's more she would have been sixteen making them both the same age at that moment in time. She marvelled at the thought. Suddenly she was overwhelmed with the desire to find her. She knew that she had grown up in Sidmouth and had even seen the very house where she lived, if she could only remember where it was. Her mind raced through every street name she could think of until she remembered, St. John's Avenue, that was it. She just had to get her bearings, then she might be able to find it. She would have to go there and see it and, if she dare, get a glimpse of GG Mel, there was something comforting about the thought of meeting up with someone she knew, even though she wouldn't be able to tell her who she was.

She walked along the esplanade, then cut across into the little town that was bustling with people and vehicles. She was nearly run over twice, not being used to the traffic and was distracted by the shops and their contents. She continued through the town looking for familiar landmarks that would help her find the street where her great grandmother lived. She even plucked up the courage to ask a couple she passed for directions and, as luck would have it, they knew exactly where it was since they themselves lived just around the corner. So she found herself going up a steep hill until she came to a large tree lined avenue and was relieved to see the sign saying 'St. John's Avenue' confirming she had gone to the right place. She counted the houses until she got to number 45, a neat Victorian house which she recognised right away since it hadn't changed much over the years, then stood outside, her heart racing with anticipation. For a few moments she just stood there motionless staring at the door, debating whether or not to go any further. She took a step forward and raised her hand, ready to ring the bell. Then, she lost her nerve and turned to walk away, only to walk straight into somebody.

'Hey watch where you're going' they said.

'Sorry' she apologised looking into the eyes of the young man who stood before her. He was slightly taller than her with mid brown hair and the most unusual shade of green eyes she had ever seen. There was something vaguely familiar about him. She guessed he was about the same age as her.

'Who are you, a friend of Mel's?' he asked staring directly at her, making her blush.

Caitlin was momentarily stunned into silence, not knowing what to say. Then she finally found her tongue and spoke.

'I'm Emily, Mel's cousin' she lied, plucking the name out of the blue, 'and who are you?'

'I'm Sam, Mel's boy friend' he replied. Caitlin could hardly contain herself when she realized whom she was addressing. For if she wasn't mistaken, this was Sam, her Great Grandfather and he was possibly the most gorgeous guy she had ever seen! No wonder GG Mel fell for him! She stared, unblinking, unable to take her eyes off of him. She had never met her Great Grandfather and now here he was, standing right in front of her. If not for him, she would not exist. She suddenly felt dizzy and out of her depth, yet at the same time there was something comforting about his presence. She remembered what GG Mel had said to her about one day meeting Sam, could this have been what she meant? Had she known all along that this was going to happen? Caitlin was feeling slightly shell shocked by it all.

'Emily, I can't recall Mel ever mentioning a cousin Emily' Sam said looking puzzled.

'Oh' replied Caitlin, 'well we don't see each other much' she replied.

Caitlin was in danger of messing up now, she would have to concoct a good story.

'Our parents fell out big time when we were little and have hardly spoken to each other since. I shouldn't really be here now' she lied, hoping it sounded more convincing than it felt.

'Cool' said Sam, 'so does Mel know you're coming?'

'No, it's a surprise visit' replied Caitlin.

'Even better' said Sam.

They were interrupted by a loud burping sound which made Caitlin jump. Sam laughed at her reaction and got something out of his pocket.

'Relax, it's only my Iphone' he said, lifting the device to where he could read it. Caitlin resisted the temptation to giggle, when she saw it. She couldn't believe how bulky it looked.

Sam pressed the small screen to reveal a text message.

'It's from Mel' he said, 'she's not back yet, she says she'll be another half an hour, do you want me to tell her you're here?'

'No' snapped Caitlin, this was going to be tricky. 'I'd rather surprise her'.

'Cool' said Sam, *he seemed to use that word a lot.*

'So do you fancy going into town, I haven't bought Mel her birthday present yet and could use some help in choosing it?'.

Caitlin hesitated for a moment. What harm could it do? Besides this may be the only chance she would have to get to know him.

'Okay' she replied, 'but talk about leaving it late, wasn't it her birthday two weeks ago?'

'I know, that's me I'm afraid' he grimaced, 'I'll have to get something extra special to make it up to her'.

Caitlin smiled, somehow she knew that GG Mel would forgive him the lateness.

'So where are you from then?' he asked as they walked back into the town.

'Umm, Plymouth' replied Caitlin, remembering GG Mel talking about some relatives from there.

'Oh, not that far then' said Sam.

'No' replied Caitlin. It was difficult to know what to say to him.

'Me and Mel have known each other for years' he said 'that's why I can't understand why she hasn't mentioned you before'.

'Well you know how it is' said Caitlin, she wished he would change the subject.

'Does she ever mention me?' he asked.

'All the time' replied Caitlin, wanting to secure her future.

'Cool' he smiled.

They continued to chat as they walked into the town. Caitlin found herself warming to Sam, it seemed that family ties existed beyond the realms of time. She wanted so much to tell him who she was and where she was from, but of course she couldn't, he would think she was completely insane.

When they arrived in the town centre they found themselves looking into countless shop windows, trying to find a suitable gift for Mel. Caitlin had a sudden flash of inspiration. She remembered GG Mel telling her that Sam had bought her a bracelet for her sixteenth birthday and knew she had to help him find it.

'Let's look in there' she said, as they stood outside a shop selling jewellery 'I know Mel's looking for a bracelet to go with her new top'.

'Okay' replied Sam 'as long as it doesn't cost the earth'.

They stepped inside and Caitlin frantically searched the shelves. There were so many bracelets of different shapes and sizes. It was going to be difficult since she had never actually seen it. She could only guess from the description GG Mel had given her.

'How about this one?' Sam asked.

She turned round to see him holding a delicate little bracelet interlaced with pink gems shaped liked hearts. It was beautiful, that had to be it.

'Oh yes' she said, 'that's perfect, she'll love it'.

Sam looked at the price tag and nearly choked. It would take all the money he had saved for months to pay for it.

'Maybe there is something similar, but a bit cheaper' he said.

'No' Caitlin nearly jumped down his throat

'Surely she's worth it?'.

Sam paused for thought, 'yeah she is' he relented, hoping he wouldn't live to regret it. He even managed to stretch to having it gift wrapped. It certainly looked the business! Both feeling pleased with themselves, Caitlin and Sam left the shop. They were just about to make their way back to GG Mel's when a voice called out from behind them,

'hey Sam wait up', they swung round to face a tall young man with a mop of thick blond hair and smoky blue eyes.

'Hi Kane' said Sam, addressing him 'what've you been up to?'

'I've just been kite surfing at Exmouth' Kane replied 'it was awesome', he turned to look at Caitlin, who found herself blushing yet again.

'Who's this?' he asked.

'This is Emily, Mel's cousin from Plymouth' Sam introduced them. Caitlin gazed up at Kane, she was not only in another time but on another planet. Why didn't they make guys like this in 2111?

'So, Emily' he said 'where have you been hiding?'.

Caitlin tried to act cool.

'I don't do small towns' she said.

Kane laughed, 'oh really? Well Miss big town girl, you don't know just what you've been missing', he turned his attention to Sam.

'Where are you off to?' he asked.

'Mel's, to give her her birthday present'.

'What, you mean you finally got round to spending some dosh?' quipped Kane.

'Hey, you know I've been hard up lately' replied Sam, 'we don't all get paid for standing around chatting up girls in the local cafe'.

'What!' retorted Kane, 'I work my butt off in there I'll have you know, there's no time to stand around chatting'.

'Only joking' chirped Sam, 'you're dead easy to wind up!'.

'Yeah, I know' sighed Kane.

'Anyway we'd better go, Mel awaits' said Sam.

'Mind if I tag along?' Kane asked looking at Caitlin, 'to make up the numbers'.

Sam laughed, 'well if Emily doesn't mind then I don't and I'm sure Mel will be glad to see you'. He turned to Caitlin, 'well what do you say Emily?'.

'Okay, sounds cool to me' she replied. She had to admit, she was beginning to enjoy herself. The only hurdle she had to face was what to tell Mel who would surely blow her secret wide open – it was then she had an idea.

'Listen guys there's something you have to promise' she looked at them both, hoping that they would go along with her.

'Wow, now you're asking, what kind of promise?' asked Kane.

'Well, as I explained to Sam, our two families, that's Mel's and mine have not been getting on for years and, well, Mel and I have been keeping our friendship a secret.' She paused to look at them to see if they were taking what she was saying seriously. They both looked at her with interest.

'So, Mel doesn't even know that I'm coming today

and, to avoid any embarrassment with her parents, it would make things a lot easier if you were to introduce me as a friend of Kane's from out of town'. She held her breath, eagerly awaiting their answer.

They both continued to look at her, then at each other before bursting into laughter.

'Come on guys' she pleaded, 'you really don't understand how serious it is'.

Kane put an arm on her shoulder.

'No way am I going to introduce you as a friend' he said, 'I don't do female friends'.

Caitlin looked disappointed.

'No, I am going to introduce you as my girl friend' he grinned at her, 'that's if the idea doesn't gross you out too much'.

Caitlin smiled, 'I can live with that' she said. Things were looking up.

'Won't they recognise you?' asked Sam.

'No, it's very unlikely' replied Caitlin, 'they haven't seen me since I was ten and I've changed a lot since then'.

'Yes I expect you have!' said Kane, looking her up and down admiringly.

'Are you sure you want to be associated with him?' quipped Sam. Caitlin laughed, 'I'll risk it' she replied.

So, the plan had been hatched, and the three of them sauntered back to Mel's house. Caitlin prayed that it would all work out okay. She wasn't to be disappointed.

As they went round to the back door, Caitlin readied herself to come face to face with her past and future. The first person she saw was a familiar face, even though she had never met Mel's mother she had seen pictures of her and so she knew who she was when she answered the door. She had the same red hair as Mel and the same peaches and cream complexion.

'Hello Sam' she said, 'come on in Mel is upstairs, I'll just get her for you. Make yourselves at home' she gestured to them all. Caitlin felt overwhelmed with emotion, was she really ready for this? She followed Sam and Kane into the lounge and sat down next to Kane on a two seater leather sofa. While they waited she looked around her and noticed some picture frames with family photos in. She recognised the young red head who appeared in most of them, it was Mel, a young vivacious girl with her whole life ahead of her. A very long life it was to be indeed! If only she knew what fate had in store for her. There was another child in some of the photos whom she didn't recognise. She wasn't aware that Mel had any brothers or sisters, so maybe this little boy was a friend. Before she could ponder any further, Mel and her mother walked into the room. Caitlin had to suppress a gasp for she hadn't realized just how stunning Mel was. Her face seemed to glow as if fluorescent, her long red hair shone like copper and her eyes were more hazel than Caitlin could remember. She looked straight at Caitlin and Caitlin felt that she might die on the spot.

'Kane' she smiled, 'don't tell me you've finally found a girl daft enough to go out with you'.

Kane, marvelled at what a good actress Mel was.

'Hey, come on, you know I'm a real babe magnet' he mused, they all laughed and Caitlin almost relaxed.

'Seriously, aren't you going to introduce us' asked Mel.

'Sorry, where are my manners' said Kane 'Mel this is Emily, Emily this is Mel, Sam's girl friend'.

'Hi' both Caitlin and Mel said at the same time. Mel's

mother asked them if they wanted anything to drink, before leaving the room. Caitlin panicked, realizing that she was now wide open to discovery. However, no sooner had Mel's mother left the room, than the boy in the photos entered. He was about ten years old with mustard colour hair.

'Jack' hissed Mel 'get lost we don't want you in here'. Jack ignored the remark and plonked himself down next to Sam.

'Excuse my little brother' she said to Caitlin 'he can't help being a pain, can you Jack'. Caitlin was stunned, so Mel had a younger brother, why had she never mentioned him?

Sam and Kane were both impressed by Mel's performance, she really acted like she had never met Emily before.

'So, Emily, how long have you been seeing Kane?' she smiled. Caitlin tried to hide her emotions when she spoke.

'Oh, just a few weeks really' she replied.

'Yeah' Kane interjected, 'she was blown away by my kite surfing'.

Mel laughed and shook her head.

'You know, sometimes it's hard to believe that you and Sam are mates, you're so different from each other'.

'I don't know' said Kane 'some people might mistake us for twins'.

Sam put his arm around Mel's shoulder.

'We both have one thing in common' he said, 'we know how to pick fit girls'.

'Aaah that's really sweet' said Mel kissing him gently on the lips. Sam reached down to retrieve the small carrier bag containing Mel's present.

'This is for you babe, happy birthday' he said, handing the gift wrapped box to her, 'sorry it's a bit late, but I wanted it to be really special'.

Mel took the box from him full of anticipation. From its size and shape she could see that it was more than the customary box of chocolates or DVDs she had received from him in the past. She opened it slowly then gasped audibly at what she saw. He had never bought jewellery for her before. She lifted the delicate bracelet from its box and held it up to the light.

'Oh Sam its beautiful' she said throwing her arms around him.

'I'm glad you like it' said Sam 'it took me ages to choose it'. He winked at Caitlin, then gave Mel a big kiss.

'Yuck, gross' said Jack then promptly got up and started to leave the room. Before he had reached the door, Mel's mother returned with a tray full of glasses and a large bottle of Coke, followed by her husband, bearing a sumptuous looking chocolate cake, which was no doubt loaded with calories.

'Right folks, who's for some chocolate cake?' he asked.

'Me!' shouted Jack running back into the room.

Everybody laughed and Mel's dad handed out big slices of cake to everyone. After they had devoured it, he decided to capture the moment on camera and asked everybody to huddle up so they would all fit in the frame.

'Now drink up and eat up' he said 'or have you forgotten we're all going to the cinema in twenty minutes'.

Caitlin found herself in a complete state of awe, she remembered the conversation she had had with GG Mel about when she turned sixteen and how Sam had given her the bracelet. Little had she realised that the two of them would be sharing the experience together and, not only that, she would actually be influencing what would happen. She could not help but wonder what gift Sam would have purchased for Mel had she not been there to intervene and how that might had affected their relationship and her own future! How surreal was that? Time travel was so confusing. She wondered if somehow GG Mel, in the future, had known that the visitor she had on that day was her and if she kept the photograph. However, for now it didn't matter, her secret was safe and she felt comfortable in that room with those people.

They all sat and discussed things in general for a while and Caitlin discovered that she had an amazing aptitude for fabricating her own life in a different era. But then, history was one of her best subjects! She was surprised to learn how much she had in common with Mel, the same likes and dislikes, similar aspirations and even the same taste in boys. All these things she had never known. How strange that she had learned so much more about her favourite relative in that afternoon than she had done in a lifetime.

Later on Mel, her family and Sam departed for the cinema. They asked if Kane and Caitlin would like to come, Caitlin thanked them but declined. She realised she had to get back to Henry Pinkerton's house before she got into any more trouble than she was already in. Kane also declined the cinema, wanting to spend some quality time with Caitlin, who he was warming to more and more.

'Fancy going to Duke's?' he asked her.

Even though she knew she shouldn't, Caitlin couldn't resist spending just a few more moments in the company of Kane. The short time she had spent with him that afternoon had been one of the best days of her life and she wanted to relish every last minute.

'Yeah sure, but only for a little while, I have to get back' she said. So they strolled back into town to Duke's, an Inn situated on the seafront, where they sat outside chatting for a while.

They talked as if they had known each other for years, and there was a mutual chemistry between them. Such a shame that they were so far apart in time. Caitlin had to admit that she was well and truly hooked, so much so that she had forgotten how she felt about Matt. Kane felt exactly the same way about her and was determined not to let her go without arranging a future date. They walked along the seafront, enjoying the late afternoon sun and Kane took photos of Caitlin with his mobile phone, photos he would keep for ever. However, time was running out, so reluctantly Caitlin told him she had to go and they said their goodbyes and exchanged mobile phone numbers, though Caitlin knew hers wouldn't work as she had made it up. She hated to do it, but had no other choice, this was an impossible situation, her life sucked!

'So when can I see you again?' asked Kane, hopeful.

'I don't know, it's kind of tricky' replied Caitlin, crushed by the disappointed look on his face.

'But soon, I hope' she tried to placate him.

'Will you text me?' he asked, his smoky eyes staring deeply into hers.

'Of course, you won't get rid of me that easily' she teased him. He smiled and leaned so close to her that they were almost touching, then he gave her a gentle kiss on the lips, tearing a hole right through her heart.

'I must go' she said softly, pulling away.

'Okay' he said reluctant to let her go.

As she walked away, Caitlin felt a great sadness knowing that she might never see him or Sam again and they would never know who she really was. It was like waking up from a wonderful dream and being faced with the crushing disappointment of reality. Kane watched her go, with a longing he had never felt before.

CHAPTER NINE

The Professor and Matt arrived at Woodbury Common earlier than arranged. They wanted to be ready for whatever Anthony Stone had in store for them. The video call had been brief and unhelpful. Stone was obviously hiding something from them and Matt had a feeling that whatever it was wasn't going to be good.

At the rendezvous point Matt left the Professor sitting in his car while he had a good look around to see who was about. Save for a few joggers and people walking their dogs, the area was fairly quiet. So that he could keep a track of the time, Matt had borrowed an old watch of the Professor's. He was extremely concerned about the fact that they had arrived 10 days later than planned. Anything could have happened to Jen and the crew of the Super Vulcan in that time. He was desperate to find out and he hoped that Stone would hold the key to doing so.

Half an hour went by and a few cars came and went. Then a silver Focus arrived and parked next to the Professor's car. This had to be Stone. It appeared that he was alone which was a good sign, though of course another vehicle could have followed him there. Stone and the Professor got out of their respective vehicles, looked around to see if they were being watched, then started to walk along one of the many tracks on the common. Matt followed, keeping a safe distance, yet close enough to hear their conversation and although Stone did look around a few times, he didn't see Matt.

The Professor was in no mood for polite conversation.

'Anthony, what happened after I stepped into the vortex? What went wrong?'.

Stone seemed unduly nervous as he spoke.

'Circumstances beyond our control'.

'What circumstances?' the Professor asked.

Stone looked around him, he distinctly felt that they were being followed, yet there was nobody there.

'Well, shortly after you entered the vortex something happened which caused it to close. We tried to re-activate it, but were unsuccessful. David examined the activator and discovered that it was malfunctioning. On closer inspection it was apparent that the integrated circuits had fused and David would need to repair it. As you know, the intricate parts used to make the activator are not something that you can go and buy off of the shelf, so it would take me a few days to put right. However, we weren't unduly concerned about this at first since we knew you had an activator at your end and were certain that you would be able to open the vortex from there and that would resolve the problem. Failing that, our future selves would be able to help you. However, when you didn't return, we started to worry, realising that something must also have gone wrong at your end'.

The Professor listened intently.

'What happened next and where's David?' he asked.

Stone gave him a sympathetic look.

'I'm afraid I've some shocking news for you about David'.

They were both momentarily startled by the sound of a twig snapping behind them. They turned round, but there was nothing there. Matt remained perfectly still, cursing himself for causing the distraction.

Stone continued. 'David went AWOL. He took off with the activator and disappeared. I tried phoning and texting him, but got no reply. His mobile was switched off. I went over to his house but nobody was home, it's a mystery'.

The Professor was highly suspicious. It didn't sound like David at all. He had known him for years; indeed he had been his mentor at university. He was like a son to him.

'Ever since then I've had the feeling I was being followed' continued Stone 'and I've received silent phone calls where the caller withholds their number.'

Stone stopped and turned to face the Professor with a look of concern.

'Henry I'm afraid I can't tell you anymore than that. I've been calling your house and checking to see if you were online every day since. I was so relieved to find that you had made it back. What happened, was my future self there when you arrived?'

The Professor was silent for a moment, studying Stone's face, trying to decide whether he was telling the truth.

'No Anthony, your future self was long dead when I arrived, you see I didn't just go forward one year as planned, I went forward one hundred years'.

Stone was shocked to hear this.

'My god Henry, one hundred years, that would explain a lot. What happened there, what did you do, how did you get back?'

'When I arrived I found that my laboratory had been perfectly preserved and luckily nobody witnessed my arrival', the Professor lied, he wasn't going to risk telling the truth about Matt and Caitlin. 'The vortex was shut off and at first I couldn't get my activator to re-open it. However, it only seemed to be a temporary malfunction and after a short while it re-activated and I was able to open up the vortex and return', he paused for breath. 'However' he continued, 'something was wrong with the calibrations as I arrived back much later than I should have done. Any idea what might have caused that to happen?'

Stone contemplated the question before answering.

'I think David may have been holding out on us. I believe he was working with someone else, someone who knew about the project and wanted to use it for their own purpose. David is the only one who could have tampered with the activators in some way causing problems at both ends of the vortex. I can assure you it had nothing to do with me' he said.

'Have you been to the Police?' the Professor asked.

'Yes, I reported David missing' he said, 'without the full details of course. They wanted to know if he had any family and I said not that I knew of. As far as I can remember, David has never mentioned any. Did you know any of his family Henry?'

Henry looked down. David's parents had been killed in a freak accident when he was a student, but he did have a sister still alive. However, he didn't want to disclose this fact to Stone as he didn't trust him.

'There is nobody, just him' he replied. 'Did the Police find anything?'.

'No, nothing' replied Stone 'as I said, it's a complete mystery'.

The Professor sighed, 'we can only hope that David

will turn up safe and well with a rational explanation. I refuse to believe that he is a traitor, I've known him for years, it simply doesn't ring true. Until such time as he does appear, we must keep our own counsel and not tell anybody about the project.'

'Okay' said Stone, 'presumably you have the blue prints for the project stored safely somewhere?'

'Yes' replied the Professor, 'I took the precaution of storing them as encrypted files on my computer, nobody can access them but me'.

'That's good' said Stone, 'and what about your activator?'

'Alas it gave up the ghost after I returned', the Professor lied, 'in the absence of David we have no way of re-activating the vortex for the time being'.

Stone looked disappointed to hear this.

'Oh, that's not good' he said.

'Oh, one more thing Anthony' the Professor had almost forgotten, 'you've no doubt heard about the sudden appearance of the mystery space craft called the Super Vulcan?'

'Oh yes, that' replied Stone smirking, 'some kind of a hoax wasn't it?'

'No, I don't believe so' said the Professor sternly, 'I believe the Super Vulcan may have been sucked into the vortex when I arrived in the future, some kind of ripple was generated by a fluctuation which caused the Super Vulcan to be propelled back in time, its arrival in this time may have caused the problems we encountered, can you recall anything which might indicate how this could have happened?'

Stone paused before answering.

'Wow, now there's a thought' he said, 'a space craft

from the future, one hundred years in the future, what a find that would be', he looked at Henry. 'Now I come to think of it, I do recall that shortly before the activator short circuited the vortex seemed to reverberate a little, but it was only for a matter of seconds, that could have some bearing on it.'

'That would suggest that David had nothing to do with what happened. Indeed, I wonder if he took the activator, re-opened the vortex and tried to come and find me' said the Professor, 'do you consider that to be a possibility?'.

Stone thought about this.

'It's possible, I suppose, that would explain why both he and the activator have disappeared. However, why would he do that without involving me?'

'Maybe, he felt he couldn't trust you for some reason, or maybe he was under pressure from somebody else'

'Um, can't think why he wouldn't trust me, so I would go with the second options' said Stone, 'so what do you propose we do now?'

'I have no intention of doing anything at present' replied the Professor 'I think it best if we wait to see if David comes back, if he has gone off somewhere in time then we have no way of tracking him anyway'.

'What was the future like?' Stone asked.

'Unfortunately I didn't get to see much of it, I was only there for a brief moment' replied the Professor 'one day I hope we can all return, but not now. I will keep in touch' he smiled.

They went back to their cars and Stone drove off. Matt re-appeared next to the Professor.

'He was lying' he said 'he knows where David is and, I'm certain, what happened to the Super Vulcan'.

'I feared as much' said the Professor 'which is why I lied as well. Were you able to decipher his thoughts?'.

Matt nodded.

'I'm afraid I wasn't able to pick up much, but it seems somebody sent him here to meet us. We should get out of here'.

The Professor looked worried.

'I suppose it's not safe to stay at my house either. We should go and pick Caitlin up, the last thing we want is for something to happen to her'.

Matt wasted no time arguing. They had to get back as soon as possible. They drove off at lightning speed, they had no idea that they were being watched.

The man behind the binoculars dialled a number on his mobile. It was answered almost immediately.

'He was here' he said, 'but he was not alone.'

The voice on the other end responded anxiously.

'Oh, who was with him?'.

'I couldn't tell you I didn't recognise him, but the oddest thing is that Stone didn't seem to notice him even though he was right behind them all the time'.

'What did he look like' the voice asked.

'Tall, dark, probably in his early thirties' was the reply.

'Curious' the voice said, 'you know what to do'.

'Affirmative' replied the man with the binoculars.

Matt and the Professor arrived back at Salcombe hill to find that Caitlin was nowhere to be found. However, they discovered her note saying that she had gone for a walk and debated whether or not to go and look for her. Matt was not pleased.

'I told her to wait here' he said, 'anything could happen to her she's very vulnerable at the moment'.

Caroline Hunter

The Professor sighed.

'She's young and foolish as we were once. Don't worry, I'm sure she'll be back soon'.

'I hope so, we need to get out of here before the people controlling Stone turn up' Matt said pacing up and down the hall.

'Maybe I should head down into Sidmouth to see if I can find her. It's the logical place for her to have gone'.

'I don't think that would be a good idea, you could easily miss her in the crowds, its busy this time of year' replied the Professor.

Matt looked at his borrowed watch. They had been gone for two hours, she could have gone a long way in that time. He was uneasy about every minute they spent at the house.

'Professor, where do you propose we go from here?' he asked changing the subject.

'It seems to me the most logical place would be David's sister's' replied the Professor.

Matt was surprised by this response.

'I thought you said that he didn't have any living relatives?'.

'I lied' replied the Professor 'I didn't want Anthony to know just in case. It seems that David didn't discuss her at any time when they worked together, so hopefully he won't have thought of looking for David there'.

Matt had to hand it to the Professor he was a wise old stick.

'Is it far from here?' he asked.

'No, she lives in Exeter so it's not too far'.

They were interrupted by the sound of a vehicle approaching on the gravel drive. This wasn't good news.

Matt's mind started racing fast.

The Present Future

'Okay Professor here's what we're going to do'.

The man with the binoculars got out of his car. He felt in his coat pocket to make sure the gun was there. His orders were to bring the old man and the stranger back with him. If anybody got in his way, he was authorised to shoot them.

There was no sign of life as he walked to the front door. He rang the door bell and waited a respectable time before trying again. Still no response. He decided to look around the back. If he was lucky the old man may have left the back door open. If not, he knew how to get in.

He peered in through the windows as he walked past, trying to see if anybody was visible, but could see nothing but furniture and paintings. Once round the back he tried the handle of the solid oak door. It didn't budge. He smiled to himself, somehow he preferred it this way. He removed the gun from his pocket and a silencer which he screwed onto the end. He wanted to make as little sound as possible, he liked the element of surprise. He aimed the gun at the door lock and pulled the trigger several times. The shots made a thwacking sound as they smashed the wood surrounding the lock, followed by a clink as they hit metal. The man with the binoculars finished the procedure by kicking the door with such a force that it swung open, smacking against the inside wall. He waited for a moment to see if anybody had heard his entry. Then, when nobody materialised he ventured into the kitchen, swinging from side to side, the gun held in front of him. The house was silent apart from his footsteps. The two occupants had to be hiding somewhere since the old man's car was still on the drive. He doubted they had gone anywhere on foot. Stealthily he went from room to room until he had covered the whole of the ground floor. They had to be upstairs, unless there was a secret hideaway somewhere. Just to be sure he returned to the library and began throwing books off of the shelves to see if there was anything hidden behind them. He derived a great deal of satisfaction doing this, so much so that he did the same with the paintings on the walls. You never knew where there might be a secret door way. However, having established that there was nothing, he continued his search upstairs. He checked under beds and inside cupboards, emptying them of their contents in the process. The place was a mess by the time he had finished. He didn't like being made to look a fool. Where the hell were they? Getting increasingly frustrated, he went outside deciding to search the grounds. He checked the garden shed and garage before venturing down the large hilly garden towards the building at the bottom. This had to be where they were. He tried the door of the building only to discover that this too was locked. Again he used his gun to let him in. However, once inside it was clear the place was deserted. The laboratory was empty apart from a few items which wouldn't have hidden anybody. He cursed and made his was back up towards the house. They must have gone out after all. Still, not to be deterred he would wait for them to return. As he approached the house, his luck appeared to have changed. Somebody was walking up the drive. He hid behind one of the bushes to get a better look at the person. He was surprised to see a teenage girl on her own. Who could she be, a student maybe? There was only one way to find out. He crept up behind her, holding the gun behind his back. She had just made it to the front door when he placed a hand on her shoulder. She gasped in shock and swung round to face him.

'Hello young lady' he said 'and who might you be?'.

Caitlin was stunned and said nothing at first. She looked at the man standing before her, he was so close that their noses were almost touching. He had a rugged unshaven face, with a deep scar down one side. His eyes were dark brown and slightly too close together. His hair was lank and tied back in a pony tail. There was something very creepy about him.

'Well?' he enquired again.

'I'm collecting for charity' she stuttered a reply. The man laughed, clearly not convinced.

'Oh really' he said, 'so where's your tin?'.

She felt the hairs on the back of her neck standing up. Who was this creep and where were Matt and the Professor?

'Which charity?' he demanded to know.

Caitlin struggled to think of an answer, but found that she was unable to say anything. The man reached up and grabbed hold of her hair and tugged it causing her to wince and lean backwards.

'Ouch' she yelled out in pain

'Where's the old man?' he hissed at her.

'I don't know' she replied, her voice shaking in fear.

'Wrong answer' he said pulling her hair so hard that her eyes started to water and she felt her self going red.

'Where is he?' he asked, his mouth pressed up against her ear.

Caitlin struggled to move, but the pain was too much, she was convinced her hair was about to come off.

'Let her go!' a voice came from behind them. He swivelled round, pulling Caitlin close to him, the gun pointing at her head.

'I don't think so' he said to Matt, 'one false move and the girl gets it'.

Matt knew he had to act fast if he was to avert a disaster. Using all the energy he could summon he focused on the man who stared back at him menacingly.

'Where is the old man?' he asked again, moving the gun up and down the side of Caitlin's trembling face. Matt continued to stare right into his eyes reaching for his mind - he could hear his grandad's voice in his head saying 'remember Matt only use your gift as a shield not a sword'. Up until now he had heeded those words well, but this time he would bend the rules a bit.

So he delved right into the mind of the man until he could hear his inner most thoughts, it was then it happened.

Suddenly the man seemed to jump out of his skin and yelled in pain as if something had struck him. Caitlin was startled by this. She watched puzzled as he stared at his hand, the one holding the gun, in disbelief. The gun was hot, red hot. *How could this be?* His hand started to tremble involuntarily and he winced as the metal burnt his skin. The pain was so intense that he was sure the hot metal had burned a hole right through it. Unable to bear it any longer he was forced to drop the gun and grasp his hand in agony. He looked at the palm expecting to see horribly scorched skin, but was surprised to see it looking normal.

Matt wasted no time, he lurched forward and kicked the man in the stomach knocking him to the ground, then he reached down and retrieved the gun.

'Caitlin, are you okay?' he asked.

'Yes' she replied taking the chance to slip away from her assailant, she had been terrified.

The Present Future

'Get into the Professor's car' he ordered her.

The Professor appeared from behind them.

'Look out Matt' he shouted.

Matt turned round to see the pony tailed man, having recovered from his ordeal, rising up ready to jump him. He pointed the gun at him. He didn't have a clue how to use it, but hoped his opponent wouldn't twig this.

'Stay right where you are' he said.

The man staggered towards him.

'go ahead shoot me' he said tauntingly. Matt froze, unable to move, his finger hesitant on the trigger, there had to be another way, he wasn't a killer. The man laughed and prepared to make a move on Matt, he knew the guy would wimp out on him - now he would make him suffer. However, something seemed to distract him, momentarily causing him to stop in his tracks. He heard what appeared to be a strange humming noise. The sound was faint at first, but started to get louder and louder and he found himself looking around to see where it was coming from. Much to his horror he saw a large swarm of bees approaching fast and they were heading right for him.

'What the hell!' he said in disbelief.

Caitlin and the Professor couldn't understand what was going on, they could see and hear nothing.

The pony tailed man wasn't about to be stung by hundreds of bees, no amount of money was worth that. He started to run towards his car as fast as he could trying to outrun them, but the bees were gaining on him, so much so that he could hear them buzzing in his ears. In a state of panic he reached for his keys but dropped them in his haste. He bent down to pick them up and was immediately set upon by the angry swarm. Writhing in agony as they stung him repeatedly again and again, he began waving his arms around trying desperately to ward them off. Then, after some effort, he managed to get up and, shaking, threw himself into the safety of his car, slamming the door shut before the bees could follow him. His face was throbbing and he could feel his whole body begin to swell up. He had to get the hell out of there. He started the engine and drove off at such a speed that some gravel flew into the air narrowly missing the Professor.

The Professor and Caitlin watched him go, totally flummoxed, then they turned to look at Matt who had a large smile on his face.

CHAPTER TEN

'So where are we going?' asked Caitlin as they drove off in the Professor's car.

'Exeter' replied Matt, 'We're going to see David's sister to see if she knows where he is'.

'Who was the mad man with the gun?' she asked the Professor.

'I don't know Caitlin, but I believe he had something to do with David's disappearance' replied the Professor.

'I have a feeling that Anthony Stone may have contributed to his visit as well' said Matt, 'he was definitely being very liberal with the truth'.

The Professor kept checking his mirror as he drove to make sure they weren't being followed. The last thing he wanted to do was to cause David's sister any problems. He hoped she would be in, he hadn't had the opportunity to phone her due to their hurried departure. It probably was just as well, since his phone may well have been bugged.

Caitlin looked out of the window as the car sped along. She noticed how little the scenery had changed, however, it was a much rougher ride in the fossil fuel driven car. The wheels encountered quite a few ruts in the road causing the car to jolt every so often. How strange they put up with this method of transport for so many years! She wondered if Matt was thinking the same. Funny that only a few weeks ago they were discussing this subject in class. She never dreamed that she would be seeing it for real. She kept thinking about Mel, Sam and Kane. She guessed the truth would come out soon about her not being Mel's cousin. What would they think of her? She would never be able to visit there again. Would she dare mention it when she returned to 2111? Would GG Mel remember the mysterious visitor? She was finding it hard to come to terms with where she was and what she had experienced in those last few hours.

As they approached Exeter the daylight was beginning to fade and the sun looked like it was melting into the road. It was a while since the Professor had been to David's sister's house, so he hoped he could still find his way. He headed for the University, a route he knew very well, as the house was in the same part of the City. They drove past rows and rows of Victorian houses mostly owned by landlords who let them out to students during term time. They turned off the main road onto a side road where the houses were further apart and larger. The Professor parked in front of a white house with bay windows.

'We're here' he said looking to see if there were any signs of life.

They got out of the car and walked up the garden path to the front door. The Professor rang the door bell and they waited patiently for a response. After a few moments they could see movement through the glass. The door opened to reveal a dark haired woman in her thirties. She looked at the Professor and smiled.

'Henry, what a surprise' she said, 'I'm so glad to see you'. She looked at Caitlin and Matt. 'Who are your friends?'.

'This is Matt and Caitlin' he replied pointing to each of them in turn. 'May we come in Sarah?'

'Of course!' she replied stepping aside to let them in.

Matt and Caitlin followed the Professor into the house. It had a large square entrance hall with a black

The Present Future

and white tiled floor and a grand staircase leading off it. There was the smell of something sweet cooking as they entered. Matt suddenly felt quite hungry. He couldn't remember the last time he ate. Sarah led them through into a reception room and gestured for them to sit down on two leather sofa's.

'Can I get you all some tea and cakes?' she asked, 'I've just made some'.

'Yes please, that would be nice' the Professor answered for all of them. Sarah's cakes were legendary.

'Okay, I'll be back in just a moment' she walked off in the direction of the kitchen.

Matt looked at the Professor.

'What are we going to tell her?' he asked quietly.

'As little as possible' replied the Professor, 'we can trust Sarah, but I wouldn't want to put her in any danger'.

'I hope you're right' said Matt, 'I wouldn't want a repeat performance of what happened this afternoon!'.

'Too right' said Caitlin, 'What's puzzling me is why that guy acted the way he did. It was as if his arse was on fire'.

Matt and the Professor couldn't help laughing at this.

'I played games with his mind' replied Matt. 'I tricked him into believing that the gun was red hot which is why he dropped it. Then I conjured up a swarm of bees which only had eyes for him'.

Caitlin was impressed.

'Wow, that's incredible' she said, 'you could earn a living doing tricks like that'.

'No thanks, I prefer to keep it a secret' responded Matt. Even he had been surprised by the results of his actions. It wasn't something he had had much opportunity to practice

Sarah re-emerged with a tray containing 4 mugs of tea and a home made cake.

'I hope you all like carrot cake' she said, handing out the mugs.

'Sarah, nobody could fail to like any cake made by you' said the Professor, his mouth watering in anticipation.

'Thank you' said Sarah blushing.

He was not to be disappointed. The cake was delicious and so light that it melted in his mouth. Matt had the same experience, but Caitlin picked at hers, having already eaten chocolate cake earlier on that afternoon.

'So, what brings you here?' Sarah asked when they had finished.

'We're trying to find David' replied the Professor. 'He seems to have gone off the radar for some reason. We were hoping he might be here'.

'I'm afraid not' replied Sarah, 'I rarely see him these days'.

The Professor and Matt looked disappointed.

'However' Sarah continued, 'he did pop in to see me about a week ago and seemed a bit anxious about something. He gave me something to give to you, he was very cagey about it'. She got up and went over to a sideboard. She opened one of the drawers and produced an envelope which she then handed to the Professor.

'He told me to give this to you the next time I saw you' said Sarah, 'I asked him why he couldn't give it to you himself, but he wouldn't tell me any more other than he had to go away for a bit and it was most important that you received it', she sighed.

The Professor was concerned to here this.

'Is he in some kind of trouble?' Sarah asked anxiously.

The Professor wondered just how much to tell her.

'He could be' he replied, 'did he mention anything about a project he had been working on with me?'

'Not really, he did say that you had made some kind of a scientific break through though'.

'Did he have any equipment with him?' the Professor continued to ask.

'I don't think so. Actually, now I come to think of it he did have something' Sarah remembered. 'He had a metal brief case, a bit like something that you would use to carry a fancy camera in'.

The professor looked relieved.

'Did he leave it here by any chance?'.

'I'm afraid not. He took it with him when he left. He guarded it as if it was one of the Crown Jewels. He wouldn't even let me touch it. What on earth was it?'

The Professor didn't want to tell her what it was, so he found himself lying.

'It was a part for the prototype of a fossil fuel free engine we are building' he said. 'A concept that could revolutionize the future of motor vehicles'. He hoped that sounded convincing enough.

'Wow' said Sarah impressed, 'that explains why he was so furtive about it'.

'Have you heard from him at all since you last saw him?' the Professor asked.

'No, not a dickey bird?' she replied, 'what are you going to do now?'

'Well for starters, I'm going to open this' he said, referring to the envelope. On that note he tore open the flap and pulled out a two paged document which had been neatly folded. He unfolded the paper and read the handwritten note, quietly to himself.

Dear Henry

If you are reading this then the good news is that you have obviously managed to find your way back without my assistance which means there is still hope. By now you will have realised that things went wrong in the lab after you stepped into the vortex. Within nanoseconds of your entry the vortex was closed at our end and we couldn't get the activator to open it again. I was very shocked by this since, as you know, we tested it thoroughly before using it for the first time. I examined it to see what went wrong and it became very clear that somebody had tampered with it. I mentioned this to Anthony and to my surprise he said that he already knew. To my consternation I discovered that Anthony had betrayed us. He said that he was from a special forces unit and that they had been monitoring us ever since we embarked on the project. His mission had been to infiltrate us, win our trust and report back events as they progressed. I was shocked by this as I thought he was a friend. We all worked so closely together on the project, sharing the triumphs and despairs, so much so that I felt we were a formidable team with no secrets from each other. However, it seems he had a hidden agenda. He told me that his unit wanted the activator for their own purposes and if I wanted to live, I should give them my full co-operation. I was totally stunned. I asked him how he could betray us, how he could leave you stranded somewhere in the future. He said that now you had created the vortex and opened the door to the future, you were no longer needed and it was a fitting way to dispense with you. He confessed that he had re-calibrated the activator so that instead of going forward one year, you would go forward one hundred years and your activator was triggered to close the vortex at your end after you arrived, then shut down, leaving you stranded. On hearing this I decided I had to get out of there and take the activator with me before his friends from the unit showed up. As you know, I have always been a keen student of Karate, Sarah and I took it up when we were kids, so I knew I could overpower Anthony. However, I had no idea how many of his friends were going to turn up and so I had to act fast. It pained me to do it but I had to. I struck Anthony on the neck, temporarily cutting off his blood supply and causing him to lose consciousness long enough for me to make a run for it with the activator. I managed to get away before his friends arrived and came to Sarah's not wanting to risk going to my own place. My plan was to lay low for a while at a safe house, a holiday cottage owned by a friend of mine, and, when the opportunity presented itself, go back to your lab and re-open the vortex and try and get you back. This was obviously going to be a risky venture, since the unit would more than likely be guarding your lab, waiting to see if I turned up. However, it was a risk I had to take. All I can do is to leave you with directions to the safe house where I was heading and hope that you will find me there. If not you must contact the authorities and use every endeavour to stop this unit, it's up to you now to try and avert a major catastrophe. Whatever you do, don't trust Anthony no matter what he says. No doubt he will have spun you a yarn to try and win you over. Please be careful, cover your tracks, make sure you are not followed, assume everything in your house is bugged. Use a different car just in case yours has a transmitter hidden in it. Enclosed you will find a map and address for the safe house, please keep it a secret from Sarah, I don't want her caught up in this.

Good luck
Your faithful friend, David.

The Professor was horrified by what he read. He turned to Matt.

'We have got to leave right away' he said.

Sarah looked at him, her face full of concern for her brother.

'What's wrong, is David in some kind of trouble?' she asked.

'Sarah, I'm afraid for your own safety I can't tell you. All I can say is that us being here is endangering you so we must depart before it is too late'.

Matt and Caitlin both looked at him wondering what was in the letter. They could see from his expression that it was no longer safe to stay there and it was their cue to leave. They got up smartly.

'Henry, please don't leave me like this' pleaded Sarah, 'what do you mean, how can you being here be of danger to me?'

'I'm sorry Sarah' he said softly, 'it really is in your best interests not to know anything. If anybody should turn up asking for us, say that we haven't been here, that you haven't seen me for weeks. I promise I will do everything to find David and make sure he is alright. It's as much for his safety as well as yours that we must maintain this silence'.

Sarah looked ashen.

'Okay' she said, 'but please find a way of keeping in touch. I want to know when you find David'.

'I'll do my best' replied the Professor, 'now we must go'.

On that note the three of them departed. The Professor knew he had to get his car as far away from there as possible, then they had to get a change of transport. He

The Present Future

wasn't about to steal a vehicle, so he hoped Matt would be able to do something with his mind tricks.

As they drove off he gave Matt the note to read. Matt could see why their departure had to be so sudden. He only hoped they weren't too late. However, as the Professor's car turned onto the main road, he noticed that they were being followed.

'How's your map reading?' the professor asked Matt.

Matt smiled 'we don't have much call for maps in 2111' he replied, 'all vehicles come with navigational systems pre-installed, more advanced versions of the GPS systems you have today. They are programmed with every existing road in the world and all you have to do is to choose your destination and they will take you there. You don't even have to drive yourself if you don't want to.'

'Sounds dull' sighed the professor 'there is something satisfying about reading a map and finding your own way to your destination, especially if you get a little lost on the way'. He glanced at Matt. 'Getting lost along the way and discovering places you would never otherwise have found adds to the fun'. He chuckled.

'I see your point' said Matt.

'Well, young man, you will have to rely on the old fashion road atlas for now since the vehicle we are currently in doesn't have GPS!'.

'No problem' replied Matt 'I studied map reading at Uni as part of my history degree'.

'Where are we going?' asked Caitlin who hated being kept in the dark.

'To find David' replied Matt and handed her the letter so that she could read it.

'Oh my God' she exclaimed, 'do you suppose the

pony tailed man who attacked me had something to do with this?'

'Without a doubt' answered Matt. He looked round to see if they were still being followed and was sorry to see that they were. A black van was pursuing them at speed and was close to ramming them. He had to act fast. Focusing on the driver he used his mind to create a diversion.

'I'm almost on them, what do you want me to do?' the driver spoke into the mouthpiece of his headphone.

'Anything to make them stop, but be sure not to kill them' came the reply.

'Roger' responded the driver.

He decided to overtake them then slam on the brakes, forcing them to stop. However, just as he was about to pull out, a bright light flashed in front of him, obscuring his vision. He swerved away from it, but to his dismay the light followed, like a search light. He swayed from side to side, trying to outmanoeuvre it, narrowly missing an oncoming lorry which blasted its horn at him. Finding himself dazzled and unable to make out which way he was going, he had no choice other than to stop. His passenger, who was totally oblivious to what was going on, and couldn't see the light, shouted at him.

'What the hell are you doing, why have we stopped?'.

The driver looked at him in disbelief. 'The light you idiot, surely you didn't expect me to continue driving when I couldn't see!'.

The passenger was puzzled by this.

'What light? There is no Light?'

'Are you trying to tell me I made it up?' the driver was getting angry now.

'Well frankly yes' replied the passenger. 'Or, maybe you need to see an optician; now swap sides and let me drive before we lose them completely'.

'Take the next left turn' Matt instructed the professor.

'Why, it's entirely the wrong direction?' he queried.

'Because we are being followed' he replied. 'I have momentarily stalled them, but I'm sure they will soon be on our tail again, so let's not make it easy for them'.

The professor looked in his mirror and noticed the black van that had been swaying precariously behind them had now stopped. He had assumed the driver was drunk.

'Are you sure they have been following us?'

'Positive' replied Matt.

The professor took the left turn and saw to his dismay that it was a dead-end.

'Great' he said, 'I should have known not to trust your map reading!'. He turned the vehicle around and doubled back, hoping to reach the junction before the van. However, he was too late. The van arrived just ahead of them. The new driver, unable to believe his luck, slammed on the brakes and spun the van round blocking their exit.

'Get the stun guns' he instructed his bemused passenger, 'this time they're not going to get away'.

'Now what do we do?' asked Caitlin, who until now had been silent.

'Leave it to me' replied Matt, his heart racing. He had never used his ability so much in such a short period of time.

'Caitlin, I'm going to try and distract these guys and I want you to run away as fast as you can. Should anything happen to us I want you to go back to Sarah's and ask for her help, do you understand?'.

Caitlin looked scared.

'Why can't I stay with you?' she asked.

'Because it's not safe' he replied, 'besides, you're a lot faster than us!'

'Okay' she stammered.

'Great. On a count of three I want you to open your door and run like hell' he looked her in the eye, trying to reassure her.

'I think you'd better hurry' interrupted the professor, 'they are both armed'.

Matt looked at them in horror, now was the time to find out just how far he could stretch himself.

'Oh my god' he said, 'Caitlin….' he was about to tell her not to run after all, but he was too late, before he could say another word she had flung open her door and was off. He had to act fast. Without hesitation he got out of the car and faced them.

One of the men was about to fire at Caitlin.

'Hey you' he shouted momentarily distracting him. The man swung round and Matt found himself facing the barrel of a gun. He focused on the assailant, who was the original driver he had dazzled earlier.

'shoot him you idiot, I'll get the old man' hissed his partner.

The dazzled man was about to follow his instructions, when a sharp searing pain shot up his arm forcing him to drop the gun.

'Ooouch' he yelled

'Jesus can't you get anything right' sneered his partner, 'do I have to do everything?'. He swung round and aimed at Matt, but was stopped in his tracks when Matt suddenly disappeared.

'Where did he go?' he swung left and right looking for him.

Meanwhile the professor had got out of the car, ducked behind it and was contemplating trying to get to the gun which the first assailant had dropped. He watched as Matt, who he of course could still see, was about to jump the second assailant. He decided now was a good time to make his move. He crawled towards the gun as best he could with his less than youthful knees threatening to give out at any time.

Matt approached his opponent, he was now only a couple of feet away. He decided to make a sudden re-appearance. He needed to use his ability to disarm the man and could only focus on one thing at a time.

'How exactly are you going to shoot me with that thing?' he addressed the man, who jumped back in surprise when he saw him.

'Like this' was the reply. However, when the assailant tried to raise the weapon, for some reason he couldn't, it felt different, somewhat floppy and seemed to be moving of its own accord. He looked down to see what the problem was and couldn't believe his own eyes, for in his hand was no longer a stun gun, but what appeared to be a small snake writhing around.

'Mama Mia!' he shrieked.

In his panic he threw the creature towards Matt.

'Thank you' said Matt catching the gun, nice to know that old favourite still worked! He swung round to see how the Professor was faring and was impressed to see that he had managed to pick up the gun that the other man had dropped. He looked around for Caitlin but she was nowhere to be seen.

'Caitlin' he shouted, but there was no reply.

'Come on Professor we'll take their car' he gestured

'What are we going to do with them?' asked the Professor pointing to the two assailants who were looking decidedly uneasy.

'Leave them to me' replied Matt.

As they drove off the Professor watched with faint amusement as the two men staggered around like drunks trying to find their way out of a thick fog that had suddenly descended on them. By the time they had, the Professor and Matt were long gone.

'What about Caitlin?' asked the Professor, 'should we go and see if she's at Sarah's house?'

'No, I think we should keep heading for the safe house now, she's a level headed girl and I'm sure she'll find her way back to Sarah's. She'll be much safer there than with us. We can go back for her later'.

'Okay, I'm sure you're right' replied the Professor, 'Sarah can be trusted to look after her'.

So they continued to follow David's directions to the safe house, hoping that he would be there.

Caitlin continued to run, glancing back over her shoulder to check that she wasn't being followed. She was reluctant to leave Matt and the Professor, but she had to remain free if she was going to help. However, despite Matt's instructions she had no intention of going back to Sarah's, they might discover her there. No, there was only one place she could go now. She had to go back to the only people she could trust, namely Mel, Kane and Sam. Though how she was going to explain what was happening she had no idea. All she knew was that she had to get there and fast.

David's directions took Matt and the Professor out of Exeter into the countryside where the Professor, whose night vision wasn't perfect found himself struggling to negotiate the narrow, winding lanes. Matt decided to take over, it would be a unique experience for him, an experience he might have enjoyed in different circumstances! At first he found using the gears a bit awkward compared to what he was used to, but after a while he got the hang of it and was soon speeding along, dodging potholes. The Professor sat silently, gritting his teeth, hoping they would get there in one piece.

They eventually arrived at the safe house which appeared to be a stone cottage in the middle of nowhere. Luckily they hadn't been followed so could lay low for a while. There were no lights on in the cottage, so it didn't look as though David was there. The directions had told them that should he not be there when they arrived, they should find a key to open the back door under a stone cat sitting to the side of it. They were relieved to find the cat, despite it being pitch black, and that the key was under it. In no time at all they were inside, now all they had to do was to find out if David had been there and if he was likely to be coming back.

The cottage was cosy inside with solid oak beams and a large log fire. They looked around for any signs of life.

'David, are you here?' shouted the Professor, just in case. There was no reply.

Matt found a newspaper dated 10 September, his eyes were drawn to the headlines: *Kennedy Space Centre confirms that the mystery spacecraft sighting was a hoax.* He continued to read the article.

Our man in the know reports that there has been a lot of speculation surrounding the mystery of the alien craft that was seen and captured on camera by numerous individuals yesterday . It looked like a Vulcan bomber in appearance,, only was much larger and appeared to have descended from space. The unknown vessel was said to have landed somewhere in the South of England, however nobody can be sure of the exact location and nothing has been seen of it since. There have been several theories as to what it is ranging from alien spacecraft, to a new prototype shuttle. The popular belief is that the government are covering up the development of a new star wars style weapon. Kennedy denies any knowledge of it, they have denounced it as a hoax and say that it was more than likely to have been a large balloon made to look like a space craft. However, we beg to differ since balloons don't go supersonic! Whatever the truth, nobody is willing to share it with us right now! We invite our readers to give us their comments on what it might be and if there have been any further sightings of it.

Underneath the article was a scribbled note, it read, *this is what Anthony meant when he said the Unit had bagged a fortune from the future.*

Matt felt sick, he showed the note to the Professor.

The Professor looked at the photograph with remorse, what a mess he had made. If he'd only stopped to consider the implications of what he was creating, but all he could think about was the potential to realise a dream he had long had, a dream to be able to travel in time. He hadn't anticipated the problems that might arise from it. Poor David had been caught up in it all and god only knew what had happened to him!

The Present Future

'It looks as though David was here' said Matt, interrupting his thoughts, 'the question is, where is he now?'

'I wish I knew' sighed the Professor, 'maybe we'll find more clues if we look around'.

'Good idea' replied Matt.

They decided to split up to save time. Matt went upstairs and the Professor searched the ground floor. The ceilings were so low that Matt had to be careful not to bump his head. There were three bedrooms and a bathroom containing a free standing bath big enough for a whole family to bathe in. Two of the bedrooms were tastefully furnished with antique wardrobes and chairs, one had a four poster bed. The third was being used as a study and there was a laptop computer looking slightly incongruous on top of an antique bureau. Matt looked inside the bureau hoping to find something there, but only found paper and other items of stationery. He powered up the laptop, but was stumped by the sign on menu, not knowing the password, that's where Caitlin would have come in handy. He hoped she was alright. He began to suspect that David had been compromised and that they were already too late to stop a catastrophe.

'Any luck?' the Professor asked as he appeared at the top of the stairs.

'No, sounds like you haven't found anything either' Matt replied.

'No afraid not' said the Professor, 'I think we should both get some sleep now and take another look tomorrow when we have the daylight on our side, who knows, David might even turn up yet'.

Matt was reluctant to stop, conscious that every moment counted, however, he was beginning to get very weary and decided that the Professor had a point about the daylight. So the two of them bedded down for the night. As Matt lay down on the four poster bed, he thought he heard Jen's voice calling out to him in the darkness, 'find me Matt'.

'Don't worry Jen I will' he muttered in response before falling into a deep sleep.

The following morning they both got up early, helped themselves to what was in the fridge, then continued their search. The benefit of daylight made their job much easier. There was a stone out-building next to the cottage and they decided to search in there. The building was being used as a tool shed and was full to the brim with gardening equipment.

Matt scanned every surface looking for something out of place, then he saw it, a light metal object peeking out from a canvas bag. He reached for the bag, pulled it open to reveal a square metal box fitting the description of the one given by Sarah. He twisted the catches and opened the lid, inside was the activator.

'Thank god' said the Professor from behind him, 'whatever's happened to David, at least the Unit hasn't got hold of this'.

Before Matt had a chance to speak, they heard the sound of a vehicle approaching.

'I don't suppose that's David' said Matt, 'stay here and keep out of sight, I'll go and see who it is'.

The Professor crouched down behind a convenient bench cradling the metal box containing the activator as if it were a baby. Matt crept towards the van that had parked on the drive, he could see that there were two men inside. One he recognised as the pony tailed assailant whom he had sent running from a swarm of non-existent bees the previous day. He couldn't quite see the other occupant of the car, but had a sneaky feeling that it might be Anthony Stone. The two men got out of the van and looked straight over to where Matt was standing, however they could see nothing, he had made himself invisible to them.

'Are you sure this is the place Tony?' the pony tailed man asked his colleague.

'I'm certain, and its Anthony not Tony' replied Stone (Matt had been right).

'Let's search the house' said the pony tailed man and they headed for the back door. Matt had taken the precaution of moving the car and parking it in the garage out of sight earlier that morning, just in case they had visitors, but the fact that the back door was now unlocked and there were dirty cups and plates in the sink would give the game away. There was no time to waste, he and the Professor had to get out of there. He hot footed it back to the barn.

'Professor we have to go' he said, 'we'll take their vehicle, I doubt they will have bothered to remove the key'.

'Okay' said the Professor, 'I'm truly worried about David, the fact that they are here suggests that he has been caught'.

'My thoughts exactly, so if we are to help him and the crew of the Super Vulcan, we have to remain free'.

They came out of the barn and made their way to the black van parked on the drive. However, before they had a chance to get in Matt felt a sharp pain in his neck. He reached up pulled out what appeared to be a small dart.

'Got you' said the pony tailed man who had suddenly appeared from the cottage. Matt tried to move but the serum from the dart had already penetrated his flesh and he found himself going dizzy. All of a sudden his legs seemed to give way and he collapsed looked into the leering face of his assailant, who was clearly enjoying the moment.

'Profess………or…….' were his last words before he blacked out.

The professor stood watching helplessly, clutching the metal box.

'Hand it over Henry' said Stone, 'the last thing I want to do is to hurt you'.

'How could you Anthony?' the Professor asked dismayed.

'Sorry Henry, but you couldn't possibly match what they were offering me' Stone answered.

'Come on, I'm getting impatient' the pony tailed man interjected.

The Professor refused to let go of the box leaving Stone with no alternative other than to grab it from him. He reached out and yanked the box out of the Professor's hands, almost wrenching his fingers off.

'Ouch' the Professor cried in pain.

'Sorry Henry' said Stone, 'but the alternative was far worse'.

The pony tailed man lifted Matt's unconscious body and put him in the back of the van. He hoped he would have the chance to inflict more pain on him once he gained consciousness. The Professor reluctantly got into the van feeling that all was lost.

CHAPTER ELEVEN

KANE THREW HIS MOBILE onto the floor in disgust. After numerous attempts at texting Emily and receiving the same annoying message 'text undeliverable number is not recognised' he had finally given up the ghost. Why had he been stupid enough to think she would be interested in him? He started pacing up and down the length of his room playing the events of that afternoon over and over again in his mind. Her smile, that hair, those eyes, the mystery surrounding her relationship with Mel - he couldn't get her out of his head! He couldn't understand why she would give him a duff number, she seemed to really dig him at the time – how could he have been so wrong? He caught a glimpse of himself in the mirror, was that a spot he saw on his chin? 'You freak!' he cursed at his reflection. Then another thought crossed his mind, maybe she didn't give him the wrong number, maybe he heard it wrong - yes that had to be it, she gave him the right number but he keyed it in wrong! 'You absolute plonker!' he shouted at his reflection. Still what could be done now? He stopped pacing for a minute and stood with his hand on his chin. He could text Mel and ask her for it. He went to retrieve the mobile, *but no*, he stopped in his tracks, supposing he was right the first time round and she did give him the wrong number on purpose – that would make him look really desperate! What was a boy to do? Before he had a chance to consider this any more his mobile came to life, filling the room with music, he rushed to retrieve it and looked to see who was calling. He didn't recognise the number, paused for a moment whilst considering whether to answer it, then, curiosity having got the better of him, pressed the okay button. His heartbeat increased rapidly when he heard the female voice at the other end.

'Kane is that you? Please let it be you'.

'Emily?' he asked in reply

'I'm in trouble Kane' her voice sounded shaky 'I need your help, please you have to help me!' she broke down into tears as she spoke.

Kane was overwhelmed by the desperation in her voice. What could possibly have happened to her?

'I'll be right over' he said with determination 'where are you?'.

Caitlin paused for a moment trying to compose herself she had to stay calm.

'I'm on the outskirts of Exeter, Pinhoe I think, I'm standing in the car park of a Chinese restaurant called the Golden Lantern, do you know it? Can you get here soon?'.

Kane looked at his watch, it was 8.30 pm, Sam, and more importantly Sam's dad's car should be home now. Sam had a driving licence, but Kane didn't, he would have to persuade his mate to drive him there – there was no time to waste.

'I'll be there as soon as I can' he said already at his bedroom door reaching for a jacket with his spare hand.

'What's happened are you hurt?' he asked.

'I'll explain everything when you get here, there's no time now' Caitlin replied.

'Okay, I'm on my way' he said, trying to reassure her. He hoped Sam would understand.

Sam, aged seventeen going on forty, was reticent.

'Are you sure Kane? You don't really know the girl – she could be spaced out' he said full of concern.

'Sam, she didn't sound spaced out, she sounded scared for her life' Kane replied 'you've got to help me dude, I can't do this on my own'.

Sam looked at his friend – he could see he was anxious, but there was something he needed to know.

'Kane, there's something you should know about her, something Mel told me' he paused before dropping the clanger.

'She isn't who she says she is'.

'What do you mean?' Kane asked

Sam hated to put a spanner in the works, but had to let him know what Mel had told him that evening.

'Mel never saw her before today' he said 'she doesn't have a cousin called Emily. The girl's a phoney Kane'.

Kane was shocked by this, there had to be a reason for the lie, she seemed so genuine.

'I'd still like to give her the benefit of the doubt, the chance to explain, she really sounded like she was in trouble' he said.

Sam was not so keen, he didn't like liars.

'I'm not convinced you're thinking straight' he said 'besides the old man won't be happy to let me take the car just like that. I had a minor prang in it last week and he was livid, especially as I am a named driver on his insurance, no claims bonus and all that' Sam tried to talk him out of it. Kane, wasn't having any of it.

'He won't know if he's kept in the dark. Doesn't he play snooker at the Anchor on a Saturday night?'

Sam could see his friend was determined not to give up.

'Yeah, without fail, but what if we don't get back before him, he'll kill me?'

'Don't worry we will, I promise' Kane pleaded with him 'please Sam, say you'll do it'.

Sam hesitated before acquiescing, 'okay, if only to prove that you're wrong about her'. On that note he grabbed the car keys from the kitchen table and they set off before he changed his mind.

Caitlin waited patiently for Kane, watching every passing car, hoping one of them would be him. She had managed to persuade a passer by to let her use their mobile phone so that she could call Kane. Quite what she was going to tell him she didn't know, she hadn't worked that one out yet. At that moment in time she didn't care, she just needed someone she could trust, someone who would be on her side. So she waited and waited for what seemed like ages until finally some car headlights started to head in her direction. As the car approached she could just make out that there were two people inside. The car stopped right in front of her and out got Kane and Sam. She was so pleased to see them.

'Kane, Sam!' she enthused, but there was something wrong. Neither of them looked happy to see her. Sam was positively scowling at her and Kane had a pained look on his face.

Before Kane could say anything, Sam quizzed her about her identity.

'Who are you?' he asked harshly

Caitlin was stunned by this, so much so that at first she said nothing.

'We know you're not really Mel's cousin Emily. So what's you're real name and why did you lie?' he continued.

Caitlin realised that there was no other option than to tell the truth, but how would she get them to believe her? They would surely think she was nuts! On the other hand, technology could help her. She took a deep breath before saying:

'My name is Caitlin Simmons and' she hesitated before saying 'I'm from the future' she looked directly at Sam as she spoke.

There was a long silence before Sam burst out laughing.

'I told you she was spaced out' he said amused. 'What are you on?' he asked her.

Caitlin sighed, this was going to be hard.

'I'm not on anything' she replied. 'I really am from the future, the year 2111 to be exact, look I can prove it'. She revealed her communicator which she wore on her wrist and was the same size as a small watch.

'You won't have seen anything like this' she said, and without further ado pressed a button on the side and the communicator sprang to life projecting images, videos and photos of her life taken that year. They watched with interest then Sam said

'great gadget, but I'm not convinced'.

Kane remained silent, unusually for him he was lost for words.

'Okay' said Caitlin 'then – do you have any water?'

Both boys looked at her somewhat bemused. Then Sam, deciding to play along, got a bottle of water from the car and handed it to her. Caitlin proceeded to pour the entire contents of the bottle all over her jeans until they were soaking wet. Kane and Sam were taken aback, the girl was bonkers. Then, much to their amazement the jeans started to dry out and, in less than a minute, they were completely dry again.

'These jeans are made of Lyntex' said Caitlin 'a material that doesn't exist yet. It was patented in 2090 by Frank Lyntex and used primarily for swimwear. Then the fashion industry got interested in it and it became as popular as Lycra. Now do you believe me?'

Kane and Sam looked at each other to get an indication of what the other was thinking.

'Okay' said Kane finally breaking the silence. 'So if it's true and you really are from the future, how did you get here and why?'

Caitlin proceeded to tell them about Professor Pinkerton and his invention, how she and Matt had followed him into the strange vortex of light that had brought them back one hundred years in time and the events that followed. However, there was still something she had missed out.

'So why did you turn up at Mel's house?' asked Sam.

This was the bit she had been dreading. She looked him directly in the eye and said 'because she is my great grand mother and I didn't have anywhere else to go. I needed to see someone familiar and she is the only person I know in my time who was around in this time'. Caitlin tried to stop the tears from welling up in her eyes, but failed and soon they were running down her cheeks.

Kane and Sam were stunned.

'Oh my god' said Sam 'if you really are Mel's great grand daughter, then who is your great grand father?'

Caitlin paused, realising that what she was about to say would come as a bit of a shock to Sam. Nevertheless, he had to know. Any more lies would risk losing his trust.

The Present Future

'You' she replied 'you are my great grand father'.

Sam didn't know how to take this he was a tad freaked out. Either this girl was deranged and evil or she really was his great grand daughter. He looked at her more closely. There was something familiar about her, yes, she had Mel's colouring and some of her mannerisms were the same.

'My god' he said, 'that means Mel and I….' he paused, 'you wouldn't be here if we…...'.

'Yes' said Caitlin softly 'if not for you I wouldn't exist'.

'Cool' said Kane, not sure whether he liked this revelation or not. Just his luck that the girl of his dreams was 101 years younger than him!

'Now will you help me to find my friends?' Caitlin finally managed to utter 'I'm afraid something awful will happen to them if we don't'.

'Yes' said Kane 'but where do you suggest we start?'

'Professor Pinkerton's house' she replied 'there must be something there that will give us some clues'.

'Fine' said Sam, 'but it's getting late now, I suggest we go in the morning'. He was still trying to come to terms with what he had just heard.

'That's all very well' said Caitlin 'but where am I going to stay in the meantime?'.

The two boys looked at each other.

'She can't stay with me' said Sam 'dad will be well tanked up by the time he gets home and I wouldn't want my great grand daughter to see that'.

'No problem' said Kane 'she can stay at mine, mum's used to putting mates up at the last minute'. He smiled, things were looking up.

'How are you going to introduce me?' asked Caitlin.

'I'll just say you're my new girlfriend. She'll be well chuffed' he beamed. Caitlin smiled in return, she was cool with that.

So they all clambered back into the car and Sam drove off. With a bit of luck he would be back before his dad could discover that he had taken the car.

'Where in god's name have you been?' asked Kane's mum after Sam dropped them off. 'Nice of you to tell me where you were going!'

Kane looked sheepishly at her before stepping aside to reveal Caitlin.

'Sorry mum' he said 'I forgot to tell you that I was going to Sam's this evening' he took hold of Caitlin's arm.

'This is Caitlin, my new girlfriend. Can she stay the night?'

Kane's mum looked at Caitlin as if she were a ghost. He had never brought a girlfriend back before, in fact, she couldn't recall him having had a proper girlfriend at all, he was always dismissive of the local girls. Maybe this one wasn't local which would explain why she hadn't seen her before and the request to stay the night.

'Hello Caitlin pleased to meet you' she said, 'well don't just stand there come on in and sit yourself down, Would you like something to drink?'. She hadn't answered the request for the sleep over yet, she still had to get her head around that.

'Thank you I'd love a cup of tea' Caitlin replied.

'Milk, sugar?'

'Just milk please'.

Kane's mum left them alone while she went to the kitchen. Her husband emerged from the bathroom, she couldn't wait to tell him the news.

The Present Future

'Did I hear voices my sweet?' he asked.

'You certainly did' replied his wife and she told him about Kane's mysterious new girlfriend.

'Flipping heck' he said, scrutinising Caitlin, 'pleased to meet you love', he offered her his hand to shake. She took it, not sure what to make of him. He had the rugged features of someone who had lived life to the full and kind eyes that seemed to glint at her mischievously. She only hoped that both he and Kane's mum would believe the story that she and Kane had concocted as to where she came from, how they met and why she needed to stop over. However, she needn't have worried since his parents were so delighted that their eldest (they had three sons) had finally brought a girl home and a nice one at that, that they didn't question what they were told.

'So, can Caitlin stop over mum?' Kane asked.

'Of course she can' said Kane's mum 'you can sleep on the sofa and Caitlin can have your bed' she wanted to make sure there were no funny goings on and since Kane's room was in the attic, there was no way he could sneak up there without being heard.

So Caitlin spent her first night in the past. At least she was safe for now, but what if they couldn't find Henry Pinkerton and Matt? She could be stuck in the past forever! How bizarre it would be to grow up with GG Mel – she might even see herself being born, could the two of them exist in the same time as each other? There were too many mind boggling questions that couldn't be answered, her head was so full that she began to feel very tired and before long fell into a deep sleep.

CHAPTER TWELVE

When Caitlin woke the next morning, for a few moments she forgot where she was. She lay watching as the sun's rays crept through the roof windows making the contents of the attic room come to life. She could smell toast being made and hear what sounded like children's voices coming from the kitchen below. She glanced at the bedside clock, then seeing that it was 9.30 am sat up with a start. She had laid in too long. She leaped out of bed and started looking frantically for her clothes. There was no time to be wasted, they had to get over to Professor Pinkerton's house and look for clues as to where to find him and Matt. She threw her clothes on, for once not caring what she looked like, which was most unusual for her, she would normally take ages getting ready. Then she made her way to the hatch which when lifted revealed a ladder that sprang open and lowered down to the floor below. She scrambled down the ladder, carefully pulling her hair out of the way so that it didn't get caught as she descended, then stepped off at the bottom only to find herself coming face to face with a freckled faced boy. He grinned at her from behind a mop of wavy reddish brown hair. She guessed he was about ten years of age and was probably one of Kane's brothers.

'Hi' he said, 'are you Kane's new girlfriend?'

'Yes' replied Caitlin, 'and who might you be?'

'Ruben' he replied, 'I'm a lot better looking than Kane don't you think?'

Caitlin couldn't help but laugh, he was very cute.

'Ruben' said Kane's mum emerging with a mug in her hand, 'leave the poor girl alone', she turned to face Caitlin. 'Would you like a cuppa and some breakfast?' she asked nonchalantly as if her being there was a normal everyday occurrence.

Caitlin looked at Kane's mum and realised that some things always remained the same. She could have been in her own home one hundred years in the future facing her mum similarly attired in a towelling robe, hair swept back in a ponytail, busily seeing to her brood. It made her smile and, for one brief moment, forget the horrors that she had faced and those she had yet to come.

'Yes please' she replied, the smell of toast had made her quite hungry and a girl needed her strength if she was going to be facing dragons.

'Well make yourself at home and I'll put the kettle on' she gestured for Caitlin to sit at the table where a grinning Ruben and another boy, a few years older were already sitting.

'You've already met Ruben' said Kane's mum, 'the other one is Nile, say hello to Caitlin, Kane's *girlfriend*' she said emphasizing the word girlfriend. Nile turned to look at her, smiled through sleepy eyes, said a brief hello then returned to his bowl of cereal.

'Hi' said Caitlin in return, feeling a bit embarrassed. She was just about to sit down when she felt somebody brush past her. It was Kane coming to the rescue.

'Right you two, haven't you got somewhere better to be?' he said with an insistent tone in his voice.

Nile looked at him with a mischievous look on his face before saying 'what's up, afraid we'll say something embarrassing about you in front of your girlfriend?'.

Kane cursed, this was all he needed.

'No, I don't want her keeling over at the sight of you chomping on your cornflakes!' he hissed 'now move it'.

Kane's mum shook her head in despair. Those two were always at each other like cat and dog.

Nile responded by scooping up some cornflakes and milk with his spoon, then flicking them at Kane's face. Kane flew at him, furious at being humiliated.

'WILL YOU STOP THAT RIGHT NOW' shouted Kane's mum 'I'm not having any of it, your dad's trying to have a bit of a lie in and we have a guest'.

The two siblings both apologized and Nile took one last mouthful of his cereal then got up and left the room. Kane and Caitlin gulped down some tea and munched their way through a couple of slices of toast with great haste before getting up to leave.

'Where are you off to?' asked Kane's mum, disappointed that she wasn't going to get the opportunity to find out more about Caitlin.

'Sam's' replied Kane, 'see you later mum'.

'Okay, will Caitlin be with you?' she called out to them as they disappeared through the door.

'Don't know yet' replied Kane.

'Was I like that at their age?' she asked herself, as the two of them rushed off down the road,

'no you were a lot worse!' said her husband who had come to see what the racket was about.

'Oh, but it's great isn't it, our Kane has a girl friend!' she said ecstatically.

'Yeah' replied her husband, 'but I think she fancies me more?' he said in jest.

'Get over' laughed Kane's mum, 'you cheeky beggar!'.

Sam hadn't slept at all well. He was still trying to

come to terms with what Caitlin had told him. Was she for real, or had Kane put her up to it? Yes, that had to be it! Kane had contrived the whole thing to get his own back on him for the practical joke he played on him the other week. He started to feel more relaxed. The two of them were on their way over no doubt to come clean! On that note the door bell rang and he went to answer it. His dad was still in bed nursing a hangover none the wiser over him having borrowed the car. So he was in the clear thankfully. However, Kane and Caitlin were about to raise his fears again.

'Hi Sam, still on for going over to the Prof's place, yeah?' Kane half enquired and half told him.

Sam's heart sank, things had gone from better to worse in a few seconds.

'Truthfully, I was hoping the whole thing was a prank' he said 'I'm not ready to be a dad yet let alone a great grandad' he looked at Caitlin, again struck by her resemblance to Mel.

The trouble was, he had no chance of convincing his dad to let him have the car, not with the way his head was. He guessed the only thing he could do was to take it and leave a note saying that he was helping a mate who had a bit of an emergency. He would have to try to explain later.

So with a great deal of reluctance he grabbed the keys and snuck out of the back door, making as little noise as possible. It took him three attempts to get the car started, *if only the old man would get it serviced!* Then when it finally fired up he over revved it a bit, cursed and hoped that he hadn't woken his dad. Luckily there was no sign of movement and it appeared that they were in luck. Soon they had left the town behind and were driving up

Salcombe Hill on the outskirts of Sidmouth, towards the Professor's house.

'Exactly what are we hoping to find here?' Sam asked as they drove up the gravel drive to the house.

'Anything which might lead us to where the Professor and Matt could be' replied Caitlin, she shuddered as she remembered what had happened the previous night. She couldn't be sure what had happened after she fled the scene, but feared the worst, that they had been captured by the Unit. She was aware that returning to this place could be dangerous, recalling her encounter with the pony tailed man, but since she didn't know where the safe house was, it was the only lead she had. She looked at her communicator which she had adjusted for the correct time when she got up, being a techno wizard she had managed to get it to work, save for the actual communication part. It was 11.30 am, anything could have happened to them by now!

The house looked deserted from the outside. They made their way around to the back and noticed that the solid oak door was still open. Obviously nobody had been back since the afternoon before. Caitlin wondered what had happened to the professor's housekeeper. Had she fallen victim to the pony tailed man too?

They started searching each room. There was furniture, books and other household items strewn all over the floor as if a whirlwind had blown through the place.

'Looks like the place has been burgled' said Sam.

'No' said Caitlin correcting him, 'just ransacked by a psycho'.

They found their way to the study and had a good look around. They didn't have a clue what they were looking for, but Kane spotted something he thought might help.

'Hey maybe we'll find something on this' he said pointing to the professor's computer. He was a bit of a computer geek, though he hated to admit it. He sprang into action, firing it up and waiting to be presented with the password command. This was the bit he loved, cracking passwords. He began typing at the speed of light, trying to break his all time record of 5 minutes.

Caitlin found herself drawn to a photograph that had been thrown on the floor. Picking it up she saw that it was a boy of about twelve or thirteen, sandwiched between a man and a woman. The child was familiar. On closer inspection she could see that it was the professor and she guessed the man and woman were his parents. She wondered if they were still alive, or if he had any other living relatives. There didn't seem to be any evidence of it.

Her thoughts were interrupted by Kane shouting 'genius!' he had cracked the password and was into the professor's account.

Both she and Sam stood behind him and watched as he zapped through files and programmes as if this was part of his daily routine. There was a lot of personal stuff, letters, photos and e-mails from students. At first it looked as though they were going to be disappointed, but then he found something interesting. A file that was encrypted.

'Hey this looks like it could tell us something' he said, 'but slight problem, it's encrypted'.

'Can you decrypt it?' asked Sam.

Kane frowned, 'I can try' he said 'but it's not my area of expertise'.

He sat staring at the screen willing it to give him the answer.

'The problem is we need the key to decrypt it and only the professor knows that' he said downheartedly.

'Let me try' said Caitlin, it should be child's play to her.

Kane and Sam watched over her shoulder as she tapped away. At first it didn't look like she was going to be successful, time and time again the error message 'incorrect data, access denied' appeared. It was frustrating to say the least. Then all of a sudden it changed to 'access granted, decrypt file YES/NO'. Caitlin selected YES and the file started to reveal its contents. Not that it helped them a great deal since it appeared to be scientific data and diagrams.

'Wow' said Caitlin suddenly realizing what she was seeing.

'You know what this is don't you?'

'No' Kane and Sam said in unison.

'It has to be the blueprint to the professor's time machine'.

'Cool!' said Kane 'so does that mean we could build one?'

'Sure if we had the scientific knowledge and equipment' responded Sam.

'You would also need a great deal of money' said a voice from behind them. Startled the three of them turned to see Anthony Stone and, much to Caitlin's horror the pony tailed man.

'you're a very clever young woman' Stone said to Caitlin 'not many people would have been able to access Henry's encrypted files'.

'Who are you?' Sam asked

'Anthony Stone' was the reply 'I have been working with Henry on the project' he smiled at them.

The Present Future

Caitlin whispered to Kane and Sam 'he's the guy who betrayed the professor and the man with the pony tail is the one who attacked us, we've got to get out of here'.

'Point taken, but how are we going to get past them?' asked Kane.

'You two try to distract them and I'll grab the laptop and run' suggested Sam.

'Sure, that will be easy now why didn't I think of that!' quipped Kane.

'Leave it to me' hissed Caitlin and before they could argue any further she shouted 'LOOK OUT, LOOK OUT!' and pointed to behind where the two men were standing. Her sudden outburst caused them both to turn round in shock. Sam grabbed the laptop and started to run towards the door and Kane picked up a convenient book and threw it at them as hard as he could.

'STOP THEM' shouted Stone. The pony tailed man sprang into action, reaching into his pocket he pulled out a gun.

'Stop or I'll shoot' he shouted.

The three of them froze, they hadn't anticipated a gun.

'I'll take that thank you very much' said Stone walking over to Sam and tugging the laptop from his clutches.

The pony tailed man grinned 'what are we going to do with them?'.

Stone was silent for a moment then said 'we'll take them with us to the base and Harper can decide'.

Kane, Sam and Caitlin looked at each other in dismay. Caitlin felt bad about this, it was all her fault that they were in this mess. Now what would they do?

The three of them were taken outside and made to get into the back of a van that was parked on the Professor's drive. There were no windows in the back of the van so they couldn't see where they were going.

Caitlin was angry for allowing herself to get caught. She had let Matt and the Professor down. Not only that but she had involved Kane and Sam, putting them at risk and threatening her own future. Plus she had decrypted the Professor's blueprints handing everything on a plate to this evil Unit.

The van took them on what seemed to be an endless journey and the lack of windows was making Caitlin feel sick.

'I'm so sorry, this is all my fault' she said with an anguished tone in her voice.

'No it's not, you were only trying to help' said Kane, trying to placate her.

'Besides' put in Sam 'your friends, the Professor and Matt, they're still out there aren't they? Once they find you've gone missing, they're bound to do something, so all is not lost'.

Caitlin supposed what they were saying made sense, she only hoped that Matt and the Professor had managed to find David.

'Where do you think they're taking us?' asked Kane.

'I don't know, but I'm telling you, I don't intend to hang around and find out' replied Sam. He tried fiddling with the door handle to get it open, but it wouldn't budge.

'I feel sick' said Caitlin, putting her head in her hands. Kane put a comforting arm around her.

'Take deep breaths' he said, trying to reassure her.

'When this bus stops and the door opens, we have to make a run for it' said Sam.

The Present Future

'But they have guns' protested Caitlin, 'and something tells me that they won't hesitate to use them'.

'She's right' agreed Kane, 'we have to bide our time and make a move when there is no danger of any of us getting shot'.

The van jolted slightly causing them all to fall backwards, it seemed to be negotiating a series of pot holes, followed by lots of twisting and turning. When finally it stopped, the doors were flung open and the pony tailed man gestured for them to get out.

At first they found the brightness blinding, then after a while their eyes started to adjust and they could see where they were. In the middle of nowhere it seemed. Caitlin looked around her, all she could see was a large concrete building a bit like an aircraft hangar situated on a great expanse of empty land, surrounded by woods.

'Where are we?' asked Sam.

'Welcome to the Unit' replied Anthony Stone.

They started walking towards the concrete building, and Caitlin had a bad feeling about it. She looked nervously at Kane who smiled back at her, trying to hide his fear. On arriving at the entrance to the building, the pony tailed man opened a large metal door and they were taken inside. After walking along a dimly lit corridor they got into a large elevator and descended several floors which meant that they must have been going underground.

They got out of the elevator and walked along another corridor until they stopped outside a room with porthole like windows. The pony tailed man opened the door and pushed them all inside.

'Ouch you thug' Caitlin protested.

'Caitlin' she heard a voice say and looked up to see, much to her dismay, the Professor and another man who looked like he had done four rounds with a heavy weight boxer. The door was slammed behind them. Sam and Kane tried to open it, but found it was locked.

'Professor' said Caitlin, 'oh my god they've got you as well'.

'I'm afraid so' said the Professor sombrely.

'I guess you must be David?' she asked the badly beaten man, 'what happened to you?'

'Oh, our friend with the pony tail knocked me about a bit' he answered, sounding feeble, 'but never mind that, are you the young lady the Professor was telling me about, the one who managed to repair the activator?'.

'Oh it was nothing' said Caitlin, 'to be frank, you made it easy for me, I grew up on your gadgets, the Beetle Bots were my favourite, I had hours of fun taking them apart and reassembling them'.

David was puzzled by this.

'Beetle Bots, what Beetle Bots?' he asked.

'Oh, I forgot, you haven't invented them yet' said Caitlin, 'in a few years time you are going to establish what will become a mega empire specialising in technical gadgets and educational toys for children. The Beetle Bots are miniature robots which form colonies and fight battles all of their own accord, they are quite awesome' a glazed expression came over her face.

'Wow' said David, 'that would make sense since I've always loved beetles, real ones that is, I've been collecting them since I was a kid. Well well'.

'Yes, one hundred years from now you are still a legend' Caitlin reassured him.

The Professor looked at Sam and Kane.

'Who are your friends?' he said interrupting Caitlin's train of thought.

The Present Future

'Oh, my apologies this is Sam and Kane' Caitlin introduced them, 'I met them yesterday when I went into Sidmouth, it's a long story, but in a nutshell they've been trying to help me to find you. We went over to your house and logged onto your computer, hoping it would give us some clues as to where you might have gone, unfortunately, Anthony Stone and his gruesome sidekick ambushed us and brought us here. The bad news is, they now have your computer and access to the blueprints for your time machine, sorry about that'.

'Don't worry my dear' said the Professor, 'as it happens David built a booby trap into the file so that, should it be decrypted without a special code being entered within five minutes of access, the whole file would be deleted. So rest assured, the Unit will be sorely disappointed when they find it empty'.

Caitlin was shocked to hear this.

'Oh my god, but what about your work, won't it all be lost?'.

The Professor smiled and pointed to his head.

'Everything is all in here, where it will stay for eternity' he said, 'the Pandora's box which I opened has to be closed, before any further harm can be done'.

'So the time travel project will all have been in vain' said David, a deep sadness in his voice.

'Not at all' disagreed the Professor, 'it was still an amazing achievement'.

Caitlin, felt uneasy, something was wrong, somebody was missing.

'Where's Matt?' she asked, suddenly noticing his absence.

'I don't know' replied the Professor, 'I lost sight of him after we were abducted at David's cottage. They drugged him and hauled him into the back of a van. As soon as we got here, they left me with David and took Matt off somewhere, and we haven't seen him since. I have no idea what they've done to him'. Caitlin was sickened to hear this, all hope of escaping seemed to be lost, and what of her dad and the crew of the Super Vulcan? Who would be able to rescue them now?

CHAPTER THIRTEEN

Peter Harper was pleased with Anthony Stone. He had to admit he had underestimated him at first, especially when he failed to produce the activator, which was the key to opening the vortex. However, he had redeemed himself later when he tracked down David Starr, the genius behind the activator. It was only a matter of time before Starr, after being subjected to torture, finally told them where to find it and he sent Stone off to retrieve it. Stone then came up trumps for not only did he return with the activator, but also with the Professor and his mysterious companion, who seemed to have the ability to create illusions. He was intrigued by him and would find out more when he regained consciousness.

The final pieces of the puzzle were about to be put into place since now they also had the professor's laptop containing his blueprints for creating the vortex. Things couldn't have gone smoother.

'What have you done with the girl and her friends?' he asked Stone.

'I put them in with David and the Professor' he replied, 'I thought they'd enjoy the company'.

'How thoughtful of you' smirked Harper, 'I'd like to find out more about the girl as she is the one who unravelled the Professor's blueprints for us'.

'Yes, that would have taken some doing' said Stone, 'she must be one of his students'.

'Bring her here' Harper instructed the pony tailed man who promptly left the room.

'Nothing can stop us now' he said to Stone, with a smug expression on his face.

'Has the mystery man regained consciousness yet?'

'No, but I'm told it should be any time now' replied Stone.

'Good' smiled Harper.

A short while later the pony tailed man returned with a cursing Caitlin.

'Good afternoon, young lady, I gather I owe a lot to you' said Harper.

'Who the hell are you?' hissed Caitlin looking at the small weasely bald headed man in front of her.

'My name is Peter Harper' he replied, 'and what might your name be?'.

'What right have you got to keep us here, just who do you think you are?' Caitlin snapped ignoring his question.

Harper smiled at her, she was a feisty one, he hoped he could win her round and persuade her to work with him.

'I am the custodian of the future' he said, 'I have the key to the vortex and can tap into all the knowledge I need to become invincible thanks to the Professor, and you and your mysterious friend with the ability to control minds can assist me'.

Caitlin felt her heart rate increase, what had they done to Matt?

'I'll never help you, and I don't have any friends with mind controlling abilities' she lied.

Harper laughed at this.

'Oh yes you do young lady, bring her' he ordered the guard, and they promptly left the room.

Caitlin tried to resist and found herself being dragged

by the pony tailed man along the dimly lit corridor. The artificial lights made everything looked more menacing. The corridor seemed endless, winding round and round like a maze. Eventually they came to a room with large double doors and porthole style windows, just like the ones in the room where she and the others had been held captive. Inside she could see Matt lying on what looked like an operating table. He wasn't moving so she assumed he was unconscious. Standing beside him was a woman dressed in a nurse's uniform

'Oh no' Caitlin said out loud.

As they walked in, Matt started to come round. He felt like he'd been kicked in the head and his mouth was as dry as a desert. He looked around him and the room appeared to be spinning. He saw several figures, but at first he couldn't make out who they were since his eyes couldn't focus properly. Then as things started to become clearer he recognised some of them, there was the thug with the pony tail, Anthony Stone and, much to his dismay, Caitlin.

'Caitlin' he rasped, his vocal chords were a bit shaky, 'what happened?'

'Ah, Caitlin, what a nice name' said Harper.

Matt turned to look at Harper.

'Who the hell are you?' he asked.

'Funnily enough, I was just going to ask you the same question' replied Harper, 'my name is Peter Harper and, before you start playing mind games, I must remind you that not only do we have Caitlin here, but also the Professor, oh and David who you haven't met yet, not forgetting the other two young men, all of whom I'm sure you wouldn't want to see hurt'.

Matt wasn't pleased to hear this, he tried to sit up,

but found that his limbs wouldn't obey him, he was still under the influence of whatever they hit him with. He wondered who the two young men were, and guessed they had something to do with Caitlin.

'So it would be better all round if you give us your full co-operation' Harper continued. 'So to start with, what is your name and how do you know the Professor?'.

Matt stared at Harper, trying to read his mind, but his head was still fuzzy. He remained silent, hoping to regain his strength.

Harper sighed.

'I'm getting impatient' he said, 'are you going to tell me or do I have to use other methods which you might not find too pleasant' he gestured to the pony tailed man who had his hands on Caitlin's shoulders.

Matt felt his mind racing, he had to do something.

The pony tailed man grabbed hold of Caitlin's hair and tugged at it causing her to wince and bend sideways.

'Okay, okay' said Matt, 'my name is Matt Jacobs and I'm a former student of the Professor's' he lied, no way was he going to volunteer the truth.

Harper shook his head.

'I think your being a bit liberal with the truth Mr Jacobs', he said holding an object up in front of him. Matt strained to see what it was, then cursed when he recognised his communicator. They must have taken it off of him when he was unconscious.

'This little thing intrigues me' said Harper, 'neither I, nor any of my scientists have seen anything like it before. On examination, it seems that the technology is beyond what is available today, so therefore, we must conclude that it, and consequently yourself, are not of this time.'

Great, thought Matt, this was all he needed.

'So, Mr Jacobs, I put it to you that you, and Caitlin are from the future and, if I am not mistaken, one hundred years in the future to be precise. Am I right?'

Matt could see that it was pointless denying it now.

'Yes' he replied reluctantly.

'Superb' said Harper, 'so you accompanied the Professor back through the vortex, yes?'

'No, we hitched our way here on the Star Ship Enterprise' said Matt, sarcastically (Star Trek was an all time classic and great favourite of Jen's).

The pony tailed man grunted and tugged at Caitlin's hair again.

'Ouch, you great turd' she cursed him.

'Leave her alone' Matt shouted at him.

'Now, now, let's all remain calm' said Harper. 'Mr Jacobs, we both know how you got here, but what puzzles me is why you came, was it a curious desire to see the past, or was there some other reason perhaps?'

Matt had a horrible feeling that he wouldn't like what was coming. Harper studied him, *if he could find this man's weakness then he would be able to control him and harness his abilities.*

'I'm a history teacher' said Matt, trying to steer him away from the one thing he held dearest. 'I jumped at the opportunity to come back and see what the past was like for real'.

'Really' said Harper, 'how fascinating it must be for you, but I don't quite buy it', he started to pace the room.

'It's the truth' implored Matt, 'it's as simple as that'.

'No Mr Jacobs it's not' snapped Harper, 'if it were as simple as that then why bring Caitlin with you and why go on a wild goose chase with the Professor. No Mr Jacobs you are holding out on me and I don't like it!'

Matt felt a tingling sensation in his arms and legs, his mobility was coming back.

The nurse standing next to him noticed this too.

'Mr Harper, the paralysis is wearing off' she said.

'Give him a shot of the immobiliser' ordered Harper.

Matt cringed, as he saw her produce a large syringe of liquid. He wanted to stop her but he daren't risk anything just yet, he would have to bide his time.

'There's no need for that' he said, hoping for a reprieve.

'Sorry, but I have to take precautions Mr Jacobs, surely you can understand that' said Harper. Matt winced as he felt the needle penetrate his skin, then slowly he felt a cold numbness spreading through his body, rendering him immobile again.

'You see Mr Jacobs' said Harper, 'even if you should decide to play tricks on our minds, the temporary paralysis will make it impossible for you to get away, so it really is in your best interests to comply'.

Matt felt helpless, it was only a matter of time before Harper got to the truth.

'Shall I help to jog your memory?' said Harper, 'might it have something to do with this', he produced a newspaper with a picture of the Super Vulcan on the front.

Matt felt sick, he mustn't mention Jen.

'Do you recognise it?' demanded Harper.

'It's the Super Vulcan' replied Matt.

'Yes, also from one hundred years in the future' said Harper, 'funny coincidence don't you think?'

The Present Future

Matt stared grim faced at him.

'So, what is it that is so special about the Super Vulcan that would induce you to follow it back here?' Harper asked him.

'It doesn't belong in this time, and I wanted to help the Professor to find it so that we could take it back to the future' replied Matt.

'How very noble of you' smirked Harper, 'but I suspect there is more to it than that, I suspect that you and Caitlin have connections with the crew'.

Great, thought Matt, he was getting hotter.

'Am I right Caitlin?' Harper swung round to face her.

'I don't know what you are talking about' she lied.

The pony tailed man laughed, 'shall I persuade her to talk?' he asked Harper.

'No' replied Harper, 'that won't be necessary, I can tell that she is lying'.

The pony tailed man looked disappointed, he liked hurting women, they irritated him.

'I will get to the truth' said Harper, 'all in good time'.

Caitlin breathed a sigh of relief, she didn't think her hair could take much more!

'What do you plan to do?' Matt asked Harper, 'why is the vortex so important to you'.

'Ah' said Harper, 'because it gives me power beyond all imagination', his eyes took on a demonic look as he spoke, 'I hold the key to the future, no, more than that, I am the future. The vortex gives me the ability to control everything that happens from now on. I can tap into it and bring back future technology and utilise it to make my Unit invincible, we will dictate what happens in this world, who lives and who dies, who will join the elite and who will be its slaves'.

'You're mad' said Caitlin.

'No' replied Harper, 'I am God'.

Matt listened in horror, there had to be a way to over power this mad man before it was too late.

'The Professor, bless him, handed me this gift and created a web which netted a big fish' Harper pointed to the picture of the Super Vulcan, 'this fish'.

Both Caitlin and Matt watched him, stunned.

'This big fish is amazing, you should see it', he said to Matt and Caitlin.

'Where is it?' asked Caitlin.

'Here' replied Harper, 'right here in this building'.

Matt didn't know whether to feel relieved or horrified by this revelation. He still didn't know if Jen and the rest of the crew were safe. Harper may have decided to kill them, considering them to be a liability.

'What about the crew?' asked Caitlin.

Harper swung round and approached her, standing inches from her face.

'They are here too, does that please you?'.

Caitlin didn't answer, she was beginning to regret that she had mentioned it, the last thing she wanted to do was to endanger her dad.

'Exactly where is here?' asked Matt, drawing Harper's attention away from Caitlin.

'Here is a disused military nuclear bunker, complete with an aircraft hangar big enough to hold a space ship, and massive underground facility designed to house a whole army for months on end in the advent of a nuclear winter' replied Harper. 'However, following disarmament it became redundant and the military sold it off for a song and I bought it for the Unit, it's ideal for our purposes'.

'So how did you manage to capture the Super Vulcan, it can't have been easy?' Matt asked again.

'With the resources at my finger tips it was no big deal' boasted Harper, 'my team in the listening station picked up the radio transmissions, and we knew that its sudden appearance had to have been something to do with the vortex. We realised that to bag such a creature would be of great value to us, so thanks to those idiots at Kennedy, we were able to track exactly where it landed and were there before anybody else to retrieve it.'

'What about the crew, how did they react?' asked Caitlin, knowing her dad wouldn't have surrendered without a fight.

'Oh, they were, shall we say, a little reluctant to go along with us at first, but they soon changed their tune when they saw our artillery' replied Harper.

'So how did you manage to transport it, given its size?' asked Matt.

'Oh, we flew it, or should I say persuaded the captain to fly it here using a cloaking device designed by one of our scientists, to ensure it wasn't seen, clever don't you think?'

Caitlin went cold, she hated the thought of her dad being cajoled into doing something for this evil man.

'So what will you do with the crew?' asked Caitlin.

'Make use of them while I can and then dispense with them when they have served their purpose' was Harper's sinister reply.

Caitlin felt sick, she thought of Kane and Sam, what would happen to them?

'What have you done to them?' Matt dared to ask.

'Do you care?' asked Harper, 'oh, I see that you do, in that case you'd better do everything I say if you want them to live'. He looked at Stone, 'go to the crew and find out which of them are connected to these two, then bring them to me' he ordered him.

'Some extra insurance is always a bonus' he sniggered.

CHAPTER FOURTEEN

Jen Jacobs was confused, she and the rest of the crew had been kept in the dark with no contact with the outside world for days. They still had no idea that they had been transported back one hundred years in time. All they knew was that the Earth looked very different when they landed from how it had looked when they set off, and they had been taken captive by some kind of military unit. When they asked for an explanation, they were told that there was a risk that they had been exposed to some dangerous substance during their ordeal in space and that they would have to remain in quarantine, pending the results of the tests they had been subjected to, until given the all clear. They had all been relieved of their communicators, so had been unable to contact anybody.

Jack Simmons and Bob Gilmore didn't swallow the explanation and had made several attempts to break free from their confinement, but to no avail. Both had military training, but nothing had prepared them for this. They had managed to establish that they were being contained in some high security unit, but had no idea why or for how long. However, all was not lost as they were soon to discover.

The room where Kane, Sam, David and the Professor were being held was just up the corridor from the crew of the Super Vulcan, if only they knew it! Since Caitlin had been dragged away, Kane had got increasingly worried.

'What can they possibly want with her?' he asked his friends.

'I don't know, but I suspect it has something to do with her technical abilities' replied the Professor, 'I'll never forgive myself if anything happens to her, it's all my fault I should never have let her come'.

'You couldn't have known this would happen' sympathised David.

'I should have been more careful whom I trusted' argued the Professor, 'I trusted Anthony and he betrayed me, now I doubt I shall ever be able to trust anybody again'.

'You can trust me' said David,

'and us' said Kane on behalf of himself and Sam.

'Thank you' said the Professor, 'thank you for being so kind to an old fool'.

'We have to get out of here' said Sam, 'I can't let anything happen to my future great grand daughter'.

'Future great grand daughter?' queried the Professor,

'Yes' replied Sam, 'Caitlin is my great grand daughter, believe it or not'.

The Professor was intrigued to hear this.

'Wow, what a surprise that must have been for you!'

'You're not kidding' replied Sam.

'What about me' said Kane, 'here's me thinking for the first time since I can remember I managed to bag a fit girl only to discover that she hasn't even been born yet!'

They all laughed nervously at the absurdity of this.

'Seriously, we have to get out of here' said Kane.

'Don't you think I've already tried' said David, 'its impossible, this place is like Fort Knox and these people are nasty, just look at what they did to me, a sack of potatoes gets more respect!'

'He has a point' said the Professor.

'There has to be a way' said Sam looking around him at the metal walls and doors.

'Well there are four of us now' said Kane, 'surely between us we can do something'. He found himself focussing on the heavy metal door and all of a sudden he had an idea, 'what about if we…..' he started to explain.

Anthony Stone was on his way to see the crew of the Super Vulcan when he heard a commotion coming from the room where the Professor and the others were being held.

'Go and see what the problem is' he ordered one of the guards.

'Okay sir' was the reply

Stone carried on ahead with the second guard.

The first guard went to see what was going on. He peered through the porthole style window and saw the older man doubled up in pain.

'What's wrong with him?' he asked David through the intercom, Kane and Sam were out of his line of vision.

'He's sick, he needs medical attention urgently' said David, trying to sound convincing.

'Okay, I'll radio for someone to come' replied the guard and he got on his radio to the medical centre. In no time at all a man in a white coat arrived.

'What seems to be the problem?' asked the medic, who was a small wasp faced man.

'The old man's in pain' the guard told him, pointing to the Professor through the porthole.

'Well I'd better go in then' said the medic, sternly, 'I can't help him from out here can I?'

The guard opened the door and the medic stepped in, the guard followed cautiously. He sensed that something wasn't quite right. No sooner had he thought this than he felt an almighty thud as the heavy metal door was pushed against him, slamming him against the threshold so hard it knocked him senseless, the last thing he could remember before he blacked out was the sound of his bones crunching. Kane and Sam appeared from behind the door, the plan had worked. They looked at each other and did a high five.

Once the guard was down, David, despite his condition, was able to get the medic in a bear hold, while the Professor retrieved the guard's gun and radio.

'Sorry about that doc', David said to the medic who was looking very sheepish, 'but we needed your help and you didn't let us down!'

'No problem' replied the medic, with a nervous grin on his face – *why had he accepted this job, his wife had said that there had to be a catch?*

'Now let's get out of here' said David, as Kane and Sam dragged the guard further into the room, and, on that note, the four of them left, locking the door behind them. The medic watched them go, glad that he hadn't suffered the same fate as his colleague, whom he could tell would need the benefit of his medical training!

'You'd better give me the weapon' David said to the Professor, 'I know how to use it and suspect that you don't'. The Professor didn't argue, he was glad to hand the thing over.

They made their way along the maze of corridors until they could hear voices coming from a room nearby.

'What is this place?' asked Sam.

'A disused nuclear bunker' replied David, 'but the person who owns it is even more deadly than a nuclear warhead'.

The Present Future

'Do you know who the mastermind is behind this?' asked the Professor.

'I've had the pleasure of meeting him' replied David, 'look what his goons did to me!'

'Who is he?' asked Sam

'His name is Peter Harper and he has his own secret army, called the Unit and their plan is to conquer the world using future technology and weaponry obtained courtesy of the Professor's vortex'.

'Then we have to stop them' said the Professor sternly, 'whatever it takes'.

'With whose help?' asked David, 'Harper has a considerable number of allies, out there all over the world, how can we even begin to stop them if we don't even know who they are?'

The Professor looked dismayed, David had a point.

'I'll have to find a way of shutting the vortex permanently and making sure that nobody opens it, or has the means to make another one, ever again'.

Kane looked at Sam and wondered if he was thinking the same thing.

'What about Matt and Caitlin, how would they return to the future if you closed the vortex?' Kane asked,

'Not forgetting the Super Vulcan' added David.

'Don't worry I'll make sure they all get back first' answered the Professor, 'but that will be the final time the vortex is opened'.

They all hesitated as they heard raised voices coming from the room in front of them.

'Just who the hell do you think you are?' Jen shouted at the man who stood before her.

'Anthony Stone' he replied, 'and who might you be lovely lady?'

'The person who is going to kick your ass if you don't give us some answers!' Jen hissed at him.

Stone laughed, *he was going to enjoy breaking her.*

'Perhaps I should explain, we have two people in our custody who appear to care a lot about your welfare' he said tauntingly.

Jen looked at him puzzled.

'What do you mean, two people in your custody, what is this place?' she had so many questions.

'Does the name Matt Jacobs mean anything to any of you?' Stone asked, looking around at the faces of the crew.

Jen took in a sharp intake of breath, *Matt, did they have her Matt?* She decided to remain silent, but Stone had already noticed the look on her face.

'Ah' he said to her, 'unless I am mistaken, the name does mean something to you'.

'No, not at all, you're mistaken' she tried to hide it.

'I don't believe you' sneered Stone, 'and what about Caitlin, is she your daughter perhaps?'.

Caitlin who's she? thought Jen. However Jack Simmons took note of the name, but thought better of it, it couldn't be his Caitlin could it?

'Well, perhaps we'd better go and take a look for ourselves, okay?' said Stone, grabbing Jen's arm. She tried to resist.

'Let me go you clown' she stamped on his foot. He winced in pain.

'Hey stop that' shouted the guard, producing a gun.

'No I think you'd better stop that' said a voice from behind him. He turned to see David holding a gun against Stone's head.

'Now drop your weapon or my old pal Anthony will develop a severe headache' he said, meaning every word.

'David' said Stone, 'you and me go back a long way, we both know you won't fire that gun'.

'Oh, you're quite wrong Anthony' said David, 'I can assure you I will if you push me'.

The guard hesitated for a moment. He had to follow his orders, and that meant some sacrifices were necessary.

'You're expendable' he said to Stone, then to everyone's shock he raised his gun and shot him clean in the head, the bullet narrowly missed passing through David.

David felt sick to the stomach as Anthony Stone fell to the floor lifeless. Then he saw the gun pointing at him and he knew he had to act fast, he fired two shots at the guard without thinking, they both hit their target. The guard stared him in the eye for a fleeting moment before slumping to the ground. A hand reached out to grab the guard's gun before he could pick it up again; the hand belonged to Jack Simmons.

Jack turned to David.

'That's the first time you've shot anybody isn't it?' he asked him.

'Yes' replied David, in a state of shock.

'Well, there's a first time for everybody' Jack said, with a reassuring tone, 'and it was either you or him'.

'I know' said David, staring at the lifeless guard. He couldn't bring himself to look at Anthony's body again, after all they had been colleagues for a long time. The Professor, Kane and Sam stepped cautiously into the room.

'It'll be okay David' the Professor said soothingly, 'it wasn't your bullet that killed Anthony'.

'Why did he have to betray us?' asked David.

'I wish I knew' answered the Professor, 'but I suspect it had something to do with money. He had a lot of debts you know'.

Jack Simmons was puzzled by this motley crew who had come to their aid.

'Who are you people?' he asked, interrupting the grieving session.

The Professor answered.

'I'm Henry and this is David, Kane and Sam' he pointed to the others, 'and you sir, who might you be?'

'I'm Jack and these are my crew members' Jack replied.

The Professor looked at them all and realised who they must be.

'You're the crew of the Super Vulcan' he said, 'thank god you're all okay'.

Jack was surprised to hear this.

'Do you know what happened to us?' he asked.

The Professor wondered just how much they knew about their situation and guessed nothing.

'Yes, I'm afraid I do' he replied, he then did his best to explain how they had got there. He told them about his invention, how he had opened the vortex in space-time and the fact that he had deliberately been sent forward one hundred years into the future. He explained that the vortex appeared to have fluctuated at this point causing a ripple in space which he believed led to the Super Vulcan being propelled back in time. He told them about how he had met Matt and Caitlin in the future and with their help had been able to return to the past. His face took on a look of sorrow as he recounted how Anthony had betrayed them, how he had been working for this mysterious Unit

The Present Future

all along with the intention of stealing the key to the vortex, along with all of his blueprints.

Jack, Jen and the crew listened, not sure whether to believe this strange man or not, could it be possible that they had gone back one hundred years in time? That would explain why so much was different and why the space elevators had all disappeared. Jen had a question of her own that needed answering.

'This Matt who helped you' said Jen, 'do you know his second name?'.

'Yes' said the Professor, 'Jacobs, his name is Matt Jacobs, would you be Jen by any chance?'

'Yes, I'm Jen, is Matt okay?' she asked concerned.

'He was last time I saw him, but now I fear he is in great danger, we must try and help him' replied the Professor, he dreaded to think what had happened to Matt and Caitlin.

'Wait' he said, 'does one of you have a daughter called Caitlin?'

'Yes' replied Jack, 'but I don't believe for one minute that she's the girl you met, that would surely be too much of a coincidence'.

'Well, she did say that her father was the captain of the Super Vulcan, so I rather fear it is her' replied the Professor.

Jack was stunned, he looked at Jen.

'Where do you live?' he asked her, realising that he really knew very little about the latest member of his crew.

'In the South West of England' Jen replied, she also knew very little about Jack's home life.

'Where in the South West exactly?' Jack asked, suspecting he already knew the answer.

'Ottery St Mary in Devon' said Jen.

'Me too' Jack said, 'all this time, I never knew, well what a surprise!'

'That's nothing' said Sam, moving closer to them, 'I'm Caitlin's great grandfather'.

There, the bombshell had been dropped. Jack stared at Sam in disbelief, this was just too surreal, he must be in some drug induced stupor!

'Are you for real?' he asked.

'You'd better hope so' replied Sam, 'without me your whole future could change!'.

'My word' said Jack, 'and who are you young man my great cousin?' he asked Kane, sarcastically.

'No' replied Kane, 'I'm just a friend of Sam's, nobody important', he felt suddenly insignificant and in awe of this man who was Caitlin's dad.

'I doubt that' said Jack, 'look what you did to help us, now that's pretty important in my book'.

Kane smiled, *yeah he did matter!*

'Much as I hate to interrupt the family reunion, but don't we have some place to be' said Bob Gilmore, Jack's second in command.

'Yes, now where can we find Matt and Caitlin?' Jack asked the Professor and David.

'Somewhere in this maze' replied the Professor, 'we'd better start looking, but we're going to need to have our wits about us since we are up against a formidable enemy'.

'Right, then I suggest that we split up into two parties' said Jack, taking command. 'David and Jen, you come with me to find Matt and Caitlin, Bob you take the Professor, the two lads and the rest of the crew back to the Super Vulcan and wait for us there. Chances are we will need to make a quick get away. If we haven't arrived within 30 minutes then go without us, it's imperative that the Super Vulcan gets back to where she belongs. Professor, I am assuming you can do that?'

'Yes, provided you can get her to the same co-ordinates as when she arrived' answered the Professor.

'No problem, either myself or Bob will be able to accomplish that' said Jack, 'anybody have any questions?'

Everyone was silent.

'Good, let's go' commanded Jack.

CHAPTER FIFTEEN

Something was irritating Peter Harper and that something was Anthony Stone, he had been gone too long, where was he? He tried to get him on the radio, but there was no response. He tried the two guards who had gone with him, but neither of them responded either, something was wrong.

He paced the room, every so often looking across at Matt who was praying that they wouldn't come back with Jen.

'What makes you tick Mr Jacobs?' Harper asked him.

'I'm not sure I know what you mean' replied Matt.

'How do you do the things you do?' Harper stopped right in front of him.

'Perhaps I will get my medical staff to open up your brain and see for myself' he said, making Matt feel decidedly uneasy.

'Shall I get the doc?' asked the pony tailed man, suddenly animated.

Harper laughed, *what an animal that man was!*

'All in good time' replied Harper, 'but first let us find out who it is in that crew that matters so much to him, then he will be putty in our hands'.

Caitlin couldn't stop worrying about what fate had befallen Kane and Sam, she hoped they were still alive, she would never forgive herself otherwise.

Matt was still unable to move, but his mind was sharp. He found himself staring at the portholes, for a moment he thought he caught of glimpse of someone. Whoever it was seemed to duck out of sight so as not to risk being seen.

Harper started walking towards the door, he had seen something too.

'Stone is that you?' he shouted, but there was no reply. He turned briefly to face the pony tailed man.

'Watch those two' he gestured to Caitlin and Matt, 'if either of them moves, or anything happens to me, then shoot them'.

'Got that' he replied.

Caitlin froze, she was now more afraid than she had ever been in her entire life. Then, just as she thought all was lost she heard Matt's voice loud and clear saying 'don't worry Caitlin I won't let anything happen to you', but nobody else in the room seemed to hear him. It was then she realised that his voice had been in her mind, he had communicated with her telepathically some how. She looked at him and he winked at her. Slightly spooked, she tried to clear her mind of all thoughts, just in case he was reading her mind!

Jack, David and Jen were just outside the door, preparing to make a move. Harper was now standing by the portholes, he looked through them to see who was there, then sensing trouble he pressed a red button by the door. An automated voice said, 'system lock down', 'ten minutes to evacuate the corridors'.

Matt looked at the portholes again and saw Jen's face, staring in. Jack and David tried to open the door, but it had sealed shut.

'Well, well, well' said Harper, he turned to face Matt.

'Somebody you know?', he asked him.

Matt remained silent.

'I think you'd better tell me, because in slightly less than ten minutes, anybody left hanging around in the corridors will suffocate, since the air is venting out fast. The only safe place to be is in one of the chambers, here for instance', Harper quipped.

'Dad, dad!' Caitlin screamed, concerned for her father. The pony tailed man held her in a tight grip.

Matt knew he had to act fast, time was running out. Jack and Jen were now tapping on the portholes, trying to tell him something. He focused on Jen's mind and reached out to her with his.

'Jen I know you can hear me and this will be a complete shock to you, but trust me, I can take care of this. If you and the others have managed to overcome Anthony Stone then nod your head'. Jen looked at him through the thick glass, taken aback, not knowing whether to believe that it was him she was hearing. Then she remembered what had happened when they were ten years old at East Hill woods, somehow she always knew it hadn't been her imagination on that day, she had heard him, and now she was hearing him again, loud and clear. She nodded her head, and he winked at her.

'You have to get out of there, the air will run out in about eight minutes, please go before it's too late. I'll take care of Harper' he said.

Jen turned to Jack and David, not quite sure how to tell them.

'I believe we are in some kind of airlock and the air is running out, we haven't got much time, what should we do?' she asked.

'There's no way I'm leaving without my daughter' replied Jack, 'there must be a way of getting in there'.

Caitlin tried to catch her dad's eye, she wanted to warn him about the air running out, she didn't want him to die gasping for breath, but she daren't move, the pony tailed man was smirking at her. He seemed to be enjoying her anguish.

'Well Mr Jacobs, what is it to be, their fate is in your hands?' Harper asked Matt.

'Go to hell' was Matt's reply, then he took in a deep breath as if about to dive into a pool of water, and that's what gave him the idea.

Harper was about to speak, but was halted by a sudden gushing sound, like running water. *What the hell was that?* He looked to see where it was coming from and couldn't believe his eyes, the room appeared to be filling up with water, it was as if the pipes had burst. He watched mesmerized as the water flowed like Niagara falls, cascading through the room and causing the few items of furniture in it to swirl around.

Then he realised what was happening, it was Jacobs, playing tricks with his mind. *This isn't real he told himself, it's all in my mind.* He tried to speak, but the words seemed to stick in his mouth. He struggled to overcome it, yet he could feel the cold water rising up his legs causing him to sway and lose his balance. He looked at the pony tailed man and realised he was experiencing it too.

'Stop him, he's making this happen, it's not real' he managed to shout. The pony tailed man tried firing his gun, but the trigger was stuck, so he started wading towards Matt. He would have to employ conventional methods and kill him with his bare hands.

Caitlin couldn't understand what the problem was, all she could see was the two men floundering around.

The water level was rising so fast that the pony tailed

man struggled to move. He too tried to convince himself that it wasn't real, yet despite this he could still see and feel it. The water rose up to his waist and he desperately pushed against the force of it trying to reach Matt. Jen, Jack and David who were watching through the portholes also couldn't understand what was happening. They couldn't see any water, just two men who no longer seemed to be in control of their own bodies.

'What on earth's going on in there?' asked Jack, wondering if the thinning air was causing him to hallucinate.

'The man lying down is Matt, my husband', said Jen 'and I don't know exactly how, but I believe he is doing something with their minds'. They watched in amazement as the two men flailed around like puppets.

The pony tailed man made a last minute attempt to grab hold of Matt's neck, he was inches away from it, but already he was too late. The flow of water increased rapidly yanking him away with such a force that it pinned him against the far wall. He grappled with it furiously, trying to keep his head above it, struggling to get his breath. This was ridiculous, surely he couldn't drown, he was only breathing air not water! Harper was thinking the same, the water was now over his head and he could barely see. *I have to keep breathing* he told himself *I can't drown, there is no water*. However, when he convinced himself to breathe his nasal passages sucked in water not air. He panicked and tried to reach the surface, but the water was now up to the ceiling. He held his breath, scared to breathe, but reached a point when he had no choice other than to try and take in air again, but all he could feel was his lungs filling up with fluid, he was beginning to get dizzy and sensed his body was about to give up on him. He was going to die because he no longer had control over his own mind. Before he passed out he could just make out something floating in front of him, it seemed to be getting nearer and whatever it was, was as large as him. Then in his final seconds he saw the contorted face of the pony tailed man staring lifelessly at him.

Matt had never killed anybody before, he hadn't thought himself capable of it. He remembered his grandad's words and told himself that, on this occasion, it had been necessary to save lives and he was satisfied that he had used his gift as a shield and not a sword.

The nurse was still alive. She hadn't seen any water, but was unable to do anything to assist her colleagues since she was totally paralyzed. Matt had given her a taste of her own medicine! Now he needed his mobility back, if he was going to help Jen and the others. He guessed that there must be an antidote for his paralysis.

'Hey lady' he shouted at the nurse, 'if you want to live then I suggest you give me the use of my body back'.

The nurse, not wishing to receive the same treatment as her colleagues, found that she could move again, and decided to comply with Matt's request. She opened a drawer in the table that Matt was lying on, retrieved a syringe and a bottle containing a colourless liquid, then sucked the liquid into the syringe. She then injected it into Matt's arm.

'Thank you' he said, and almost immediately felt the sensation coming back. Within seconds he could move his hands and feet, then his whole body came back to life. He sat up and jumped off of the table.

Caitlin was relieved.

'Let's get out of here' he said, Caitlin needed no persuasion.

Caroline Hunter

They ran to the door and tried to open it, but it was stuck. Jack, Jen and David were beginning to suffer from the symptoms of thinning air and their movements were getting sluggish.

'There has to be a way of overriding the lock' said Matt. He started looking for a control panel on the wall, but could see nothing obvious.

Jen looked through the porthole at Matt, longing to reach him, but feeling helpless. She was getting dizzy and wondered how much time she had left. How awful to die so close to the one you loved, unable to touch them one last time.

Jack and David had tried to find another way out, but the corridor was sealed off, they were trapped.

Caitlin pressed her face up against the glass and stared into the misty eyes of her father.

'Dad, dad' she shouted, then turned to Matt, 'please Matt, we've got to help them'.

Matt felt helpless, his gift couldn't help them now, what was he to do?

'Caitlin' he said, trying to sound calm, 'you're the one with the technical skills, can't you see anything that could override the locking system?'

Caitlin looked around the room in desperation, there had to be something. Then she spotted it, a black box on the far wall. Without hesitating she ran over to it and opened the hinged lid. Inside she found a computerised control panel. There was no time to waste, she got to work, furiously pressing the keys, whizzing through each menu, trying to find the one that would help them.

'Come on!' she shouted at it, 'show me'.

Matt watched her, then looked to see if Jen was still okay. He couldn't see her face at the portholes anymore.

He ran over and looked through the glass only to see her and the other two slumped on the floor, not moving.

'Jen don't give up, please' he tried to reach her mind, but she didn't stir.

'Caitlin, we're running out of time' he shouted, afraid they were already too late.

'I'm trying' shrieked Caitlin, her hands were moving faster than the computer could keep up with her, then, all of a sudden, there was a buzz and the door locks unsealed.

'System override operated' the automated voice said, 'air will be restored to the non essential areas'.

Matt wasted no time opening the door, he had to get to Jen and get some air into her lungs. Caitlin was right behind him, praying that her dad was still alive.

Matt dropped to his knees, grabbed hold of Jen and pulled her close to him to see if she was still breathing and found much to his relief that she was.

'Jen' he said, 'Jen, are you okay?'

She opened her eyes and said in little more than a whisper, 'yes'.

'Dad' said Caitlin, shaking his shoulders, 'dad, speak to me'.

Jack Simmons smiled at his daughter, 'Caitlin what the hell are you doing here?' he asked.

'Never mind that now' she replied with relief, 'we need to find the Professor and my friends'.

Jack looked at his watch and was suddenly galvanized into action.

'They should be back at the Super Vulcan' he said, 'and we had better get there ourselves since I instructed them to leave without us if we didn't arrive in…' he worked out the time left before saying 'five minutes from now'.

'Come on then' said Matt, he looked at David who was taking in deep breaths of air.

'Are you okay?' he asked

'Yes, thanks for asking' replied David, 'and thanks for bringing the Professor back' he added.

'Oh, you must be David' said Matt (they hadn't yet been introduced), 'pleased to meet you at last'.

'Likewise' said David.

'Come on let's go!' said Caitlin, anxious not to be left behind. On that note, they all headed off down the maze of corridors until they reached the elevator they had arrived in. They took the elevator up to the surface and headed towards the aircraft hanger, and there in all its glory was the Super Vulcan.

'Wow' said David 'so this is the future of space travel'. He marvelled at the sheer size of it. Before anyone else had the chance to speak, a door shaped hole appeared in the fuselage and steps magically rolled out all the way to the ground as if inviting them to go on board.

'After you' Jack gestured to the others.

So they climbed swiftly up the steps to the top, then through the door into the pristine interior.

Caitlin, David and Matt, having never been inside it before were amazed at the spaciousness. The interior was designed as much for comfort as for practicality. There were individual sleeping quarters for the crew as well as communal recreation areas including a gym. Then there was a menagerie, complete with a selection of animals, and a botanical garden, it was like Noah's ark! There was everything on board needed to keep going for an eternity without the worry of running out of supplies, they had the facility to grow their own. The cockpit was the ultimate in design kitted out with all sorts of equipment and instruments that they had never seen the like of before. It was an amazing feat of engineering. Everything was so lightweight and compact, designed to provide flawless aerodynamics with the ability to harness the power of the sun.

'This has to be seen to be believed' uttered David in a state of awe.

'My thoughts exactly' said the Professor, as they joined him and the others in one of the passenger cabins.

Caitlin was delighted to see Kane and Sam alive and well and they were equally glad to see that she had come to no harm.

Sam was transfixed. There he was looking at his future family, none of whom would exist without him, it was awesome! Yet it could all have gone so horribly wrong, supposing he had been killed, would they all have simply ceased to exist? He felt as if so much was resting on his shoulders now, but he was only seventeen, such responsibility was overwhelming!

Kane had mixed emotions. For the first time in his life he had met someone who made him feel alive and protective, he so wanted to give Caitlin a big hug, yet something was holding him back. Was it that he was numbed by the enormity of the whole thing, or was it that he was saddened by what he knew was to come, an eternity without her. *My life sucks* he thought to himself. How was he going to explain this to his mum who had been so made up to see him with a girlfriend?

'Thank you for taking good care of my daughter, all of you' Jack interrupted his thoughts 'but now we have to get out of this mess?'

Matt looked at the professor.

'Okay professor, what do you suggest?' he asked.

The professor was deep in thought.

'I need everybody to be in exactly the same position as they were at the time they entered the vortex' he said 'but first I need to get back to my lab, can you manage that Jack?' he asked.

'No problem' replied Jack, 'everybody take your seats for the ride of your life'.

'Cool' said Kane, 'I'm going for a trip in a space ship'.

'I'm afraid we won't be leaving the Earth's orbit on this trip' said Jack.

'No worries' said Kane, 'it's still going to be fantastic'.

CHAPTER SIXTEEN

Much to the relief of Jack, his crew and passengers, the Super Vulcan took off effortlessly and in no time at all was soaring through the sky at the speed of sound. Kane was thrilled by the experience, as a child he had dreamed of going into space and, although he wasn't going to do that on this occasion, he was at least being treated to a flight in a space craft, the next best thing. Caitlin held on tight to his hand, unlike her dad, she had no head for flying and wasn't really enjoying the experience. Jen nuzzled up to Matt, she was proud of what he had done, coming to her rescue. However, there was still a lot of explaining for him to do, she always knew he had special abilities, but hadn't witnessed them quite like that before. Matt was struggling to come to terms with having killed two men, he shut his eyes and found himself drifting back in time to the night his grandad had first told him about his gift.

'Matt' his grandad was looking him in the eye sternly, 'there may come a time when you have to use your gift as a weapon, to save yourself or others. However, you must promise me that you won't make the same mistake as I'.

'What mistake grandad?' Matt asked, wondering how this gentle old man could ever have done anything wrong. His grandad looked pained when he spoke.

'There was once a time, when I was much younger' he said, 'when I was in my twenties and out late one night' he continued. Matt struggled to picture his grandad as a young man.

Caroline Hunter

'I had been to a night club in Exeter with my friends and was on my way home. The streets were full of other young people, staggering out of pubs and clubs, a little worse for wear from too much drink. I was quite sober, on account of the fact that alcohol didn't agree with me, also the gift can be dangerous if exercised with an unclear mind'. Matt stared up at his grandad, wondering what was coming next.

'Anyway' his grandad continued, 'I was walking along by the quay side, minding my own business when, all of a sudden, this lad jumped out in front of me. At first he said nothing, just stood there looking me up and down. I politely asked him to step aside and let me pass, but he seemed to take offence at this and said he was going to teach me a lesson. He reached into his pocket and retrieved a knife. Before I could say another word he lurched right at me, slashing my arm with the knife. I remember looking down at the blood seeping out of the wound in disbelief. I looked up at the lad who was just standing there, taunting me, brandishing the knife like some kind of Samurai. Then, something happened to me, it was as if somebody had unleashed a demon within me. I felt myself getting angry, very angry, and to make matters worse, the lad started laughing at me. It was then that I struck, using the full force of my abilities. I made the lad believe that the earth was opening up under his feet. I remember the look of horror in his eyes as he stared in disbelief at the ground. He started to back away from where the crack was appearing, moving further and further towards the river. He glanced up at me, as if to ask for help, yet didn't utter a word. I was in a trance like state, all I could think about was getting rid of this horrible creep before he could do me any more harm. I watched as he backed perilously close to the edge, shaking in fear, then, before I could do anything, his feet got caught up in a large chain and he tripped falling backwards into the river. Everything seemed to happen in slow motion from then on. I heard a loud splash as he hit the water and that seemed to break the trance. Shocked by what I had done, I was suddenly galvanised into action. I ran over to the river's edge frantically looking to see him surface. However, he did not. I ran along the river in case the current had dragged him further, but he still failed to materialise. I decided to go and get help, but it was some time before I found anybody sober enough to assist. By then, it was too late, the lad had failed to surface and couldn't be seen. His body was found the next day by some fishermen. I never got over what I had done'. Matt's heart went out to his grandad.

'You were only trying to save yourself' he said, trying to reassure him.

'No lad' his grandad begged to differ, 'I gave into the gift and lost control of my better judgment', he stared at Matt an ominous look in his eyes, 'you must never let that happen to you Matt' he said, 'a heavy heart is hard to live with'.

'Sorry grandad' Matt said out loud to himself, coming back to the present. Jen looked at him puzzled.

'What was that?' she asked

'Nothing' he replied, smiling at her, 'just a bad memory coming back to haunt me'.

The Professor and David were busy discussing the monumental task ahead of them, they had a big responsibility now to put things right, it was crucial that they got the timings spot on.

In what seemed like no time at all the Super Vulcan started to descend and landed at sea, a few miles from the shore, below where the Professor's estate was. A state of the art inflatable rib was deployed to drop the passengers off, before the Super Vulcan could begin her voyage home. Caitlin and Matt said goodbye to Jack and Jen, they would have to make their way back via the Professor's lab, while the Super Vulcan would need to head off into orbit and position itself where it could enter the vortex in space.

So the Professor and the others watched as the magnificent craft took off and headed off to sea before launching into space, causing a bit of a stir to say the least. The latest sighting of the Super Vulcan would no doubt be all over the news for the next few days, then, after it disappeared without a trace, would soon be forgotten about and become yet another one of life's many unsolved mysteries.

Caitlin was going to find it hard to say her goodbyes to Kane and Sam. She had grown very fond of them both. She would have loved to see Mel again, but sadly that wasn't going to be an option now. She wondered how it would be when she next saw GG in her own time. Sam didn't think Mel would believe him if he told her the truth about who Caitlin really was, so said that he would probably make some other story up. Kane hadn't worked out quite what he would tell his mum, but he knew his life would never be the same again.

'I'm really going to miss you, its been awesome' he said to Caitlin too shy to say what he really felt.

'Me too' replied Caitlin trying not to get too emotional about the whole thing. 'You could leave me some kind of a message to let me know how things turn out', she added.

Kane grinned 'Oh what and bury it by a tree in the back garden!'

'How about a time capsule?' suggested Caitlin light heartedly 'you could leave a lock of hair and some mementoes'

'You've got to be kidding' quipped Sam 'a lock of that hair would develop a life of its own and grow like a giant hairball, sprouting like a fungus through the earth!'

They all laughed, then Sam looked serious.

'Do we have a good life together Mel and me?' he dared to ask Caitlin.

Caitlin smiled a reassuring smile.

'Absolutely brilliant' was her succinct reply 'that's all I'm going to say, other than give her my love when you next see her, even though I know you can't'.

'Okay' replied Sam 'maybe some day I'll tell her who you really are, when we're old and grey and I think she can take it'.

Caitlin smiled, she was only sorry that Sam would not be there with GG when she returned.

'Caitlin we have to go now' Matt interrupted her thoughts.

They were all back at the professor's house, the warm September sun made everything seem perfectly normal. Nobody could have known that this odd assortment of individuals all came from different eras. Sam and Kane accompanied Caitlin to the Professor's laboratory so that they could see the vortex with their own eyes, it would give them some kind of closure on the whole adventure.

The Professor and David were checking last minute details, they had to make sure they got the calibrations spot on. The vortex was still closed off at that point and the laboratory was reasonably silent. Then, once everything was ready, David engaged the activator and opened it up. All of a sudden the peace and quiet was disrupted by what sounded like a jet engine starting up, and everybody was momentarily startled. Kane and Sam stared at the vortex in amazement, they had never seen anything like it.

'Wow, that's amazing' said Sam

'Cool' said Kane, mesmerized by the swirling rays of light.

'Caitlin are you ready?' asked the Professor

Caitlin looked at the vortex nervously. David was going to travel with her to make sure she went to the right point in time, then he would return to let everybody know she was okay. Matt would apparently be following later, he had one more issue to sort out first, though he and the Professor didn't seem able to agree over whatever it was.

'Come on Caitlin' David gestured to her.

Caitlin took a deep breath then gave Kane and Sam a big hug before turning and walking towards the vortex.

'Wait' shouted Kane, then without a moment's hesitation, he ran to Caitlin, swung her round to face him and before she could protest, gave her a long, lingering kiss, not caring what anybody else thought. As he pulled her close to him, Caitlin felt as if she was melting, and wished that time would stand still for them.

'I want you to have this' Kane said softly handing her a pebble. On looking at it she could see that it was no ordinary pebble for there was something inscribed on it. She read the inscription, it said simply *'remember me, I'll never forget you, luv Kane xx'*.

She smiled and put it in her pocket.

'I'll treasure it' she said before stepping into the vortex with David. As she felt herself being swept up by the force of it she managed one last backward glance and could have sworn she saw a tear in Kane's eye.

Meanwhile, Jack Simmons had positioned the Super Vulcan at the exact co-ordinates given to him by the Professor, but there was no sign of the vortex.

'Come on where are you?' he said, they had got this far, this should be the easy part now. He and Bob scanned the area, but could see nothing but stars and darkness. Then all of a sudden, they seemed to encounter some turbulence, much like they had done before.

'Hey, look over there' said Bob, pointing in the direction of a bright light.

'There it is' said Jack, steering the Super Vulcan towards the swirling tunnel of light.

'Brace yourselves crew' he announced over the intercom.

Jen tensed up, she hoped everything would go to plan and she would soon be back with Matt again in their own home. She hadn't lost her desire for space travel, but was happy to put it on hold for a while. She looked at the rest of the crew and wondered what they were thinking, would they have reservations about carrying on with the mission?

The Super Vulcan started vibrating and everybody held their breath as it entered the vortex. Jen felt as if she was on a fair ground ride as the vortex spun the giant craft round and round until finally depositing it back into space, one hundred years in the future. Jack and Bob were relieved to see the familiar sight of the space elevators once more and even more relieved when they made contact with mission control, and found that they had returned just a few moments after they left. They would have some explaining to do, however, the truth could never be told. The Professor's time machine would forever have to remain a secret if the future was to be safeguarded. After being satisfied that the Super Vulcan and Caitlin had been returned to the right moment in time, David went back to inform the Professor and Matt.

CHAPTER SEVENTEEN

PART THREE

BACK TO THE FUTURE, ONE HUNDRED YEARS LATER

Everything looked normal at the Simmons household when Caitlin returned, the party had long finished and her mother and sister were clearing up.

'Where have you been?' Karel asked her wayward daughter.

'Oh, I went to hear one of my teachers talking about the human psyche at the Henry Pinkerton museum' she replied, that part was certainly true.

'Really, was it interesting?' Karel asked, surprised at this revelation.

'It was okay I suppose' replied Caitlin, not wanting to sound too keen, god forbid that her mother should ask her to go into any more detail since it seemed like a long time to her since she attended the talk. It was hard to get her head around the fact that she had lived a few more days in the seconds she had been gone.

Everything was just as she had left it, but her life would never be the same again, not after what she had been through. The good news was that there were two people she could share her secret with, her dad and Matt Jacobs, but nobody else could ever know, she had been sworn to secrecy. It was going to be hard keeping it from her best friend Michaela, but she must. However, there was still one person who may know the truth and she was going to find out very soon.

The next morning, her mother had some good news for her.

'Cait' she said, her face glowing with happiness, 'you'll never guess what'

'What?' asked Caitlin, even though she could guess what was coming.

'it's your dad, we just had a call to say he's coming home'

Caitlin tried to act surprised.

'That's great news' she enthused 'but what about the Super Vulcan mission into deep space?'

'The mission has been postponed until a later date'

Caitlin was so pleased for her mum, she knew how hard it had been for her.

'Oh wow', she said, 'but why?'.

'I've no idea, I guess your dad will fill us in on the details when we see him'.

'So what happens now?' asked Caitlin

'They are returning to earth, they need to make sure the Super Vulcan hasn't sustained any serious damage before it can continue its journey. That means your dad will be able to spend some quality time with us, oh Cait I'm so happy' she beamed.

'Me too' replied Caitlin, though she was still sad about one thing. She would never see Kane again. She reached into her pocket and retrieved the pebble, it was the only thing she had left of him, *unless*..... there was something she had to do.

'Mum I'm just popping across to see GG' she said

'Okay, tell her she's expected for dinner later in case

she has forgotten – you know how bad her memory can be' said Karel, still basking in the news.

So Caitlin walked the familiar path to GG's annex. She had never felt so anxious before, it was like she was walking into the unknown. Would GG know? Nervously she knocked on the door and waited. After a few moments she could see the familiar shape of GG shuffling along. The door opened and there stood Mel, her face still recognisable from the girl she had once been. The wonders of modern science had helped her to retain such a youthful appearance.

'Cait, or should I say Emily' she greeted her, 'I've been expecting you, do come in' she stepped aside to let her Great Grand daughter in.

'Can I get you a nice cup of tea my dear, I think you need it after what you have been through' she said a knowing look on her face.

Caitlin was stunned, *she knew.*

GG smiled at her. 'I think you'd better sit down, we have so much to talk about, and I have something to show you'.

Caitlin sat down and listened while GG explained what had happened after she left one hundred years ago.

'Sam told me everything' she said, 'oh he tried to give me some cock and bull story at first, but I could always tell when he was lying' she sighed. 'So he told me the truth, though it took some time to sink in, and I was totally shocked by it all. However, when I thought about it I could see the resemblance in you' she paused to look at her Great Grand daughter. How she had waited and longed for this day to come.

'So Sam and I made sure we kept the family line going and got married five years later. I remember how excited

I was the day you were born, such a rosy cheeked baby, how lovely you were. It was me who suggested that you be called Caitlin' she chuckled at this, 'funny how things turn out'. Before Caitlin could say anything in response to this, Mel got up.

'Wait here dear, I'll be back shortly with some tea and a surprise' she left the room and Caitlin wondered what the surprise was. A few minutes later she found out. Mel returned and produced a faded photograph. She recognised it immediately, it was the one that had been taken at Mel's house in Sidmouth. There they all were, Caitlin, Mel, Sam and Kane, four teenagers huddled up together. She felt a pang of sadness on seeing it. There were so many questions she had to ask, yet she was afraid of what the answers might be. She started with the least painful but most puzzling.

'What happened to your brother Jack, and why did you never tell us about him?' she asked.

Mel looked sad for a moment.

'Dear Jack, I'd almost forgotten him' she said with a sigh. 'Sadly Jack died two years after that day' she paused, her face full of pain. 'He was run over by a car whilst cycling to the park, it was a terrible tragedy, one that mum and dad never got over' she took a large sip of tea 'we couldn't bear to talk about it any, of us, not for a long time', her eyes had a glazed look in them. Caitlin was shocked by this revelation, she could still see the cheeky grin on Jack's face, how unbearable it must have been for the family.

'Oh GG I'm so sorry" said Caitlin, she leaned forward and gave Mel a big hug.

'But why did you keep it a secret from us?' she asked.

'I don't know' was Mel's reply, 'I suppose it was less painful that way'. She dabbed at the tears that were forming in her eyes.

Caitlin could hardly breathe when she asked the next question.

'What happened to Kane?' there she had said it.

Mel smiled at her, *poor kid, how hard this must be for her to take in.*

'Kane, oh yes' said Mel 'seems such a long time ago now' she looked at Caitlin's anxious face. 'He never forgot you, you know, kept the mobile phone with your photos in all his life. He and Sam remained friends throughout their lives, and after Sam died he was of great comfort to me' she smiled at the memory. Caitlin was dreading the next bit.

'Did he find somebody else, get married?' she asked

'Oh yes' replied Mel 'he married a lovely girl called Jasmina and they had three sons. Funny thing is Jasmina was a lot like you' she hoped these words might be of some comfort. Caitlin found it all too painful, but what else did she expect?

'Is he still alive?' she dared to ask

'No' replied Mel sadly, 'he died fourteen years ago when you were just a child'.

Caitlin wanted to cry, but couldn't, somehow it didn't seem real. Her Kane was still out there somewhere, seventeen and very much alive and that was how she would remember him.

'You did meet him again you know' said Mel to Caitlin's surprise.

'What, when?' she asked, she could only have been a very small child.

'Shortly before he died, when you were just two, he

came to visit me and I introduced you, though you won't remember. He looked so sad, yet at the same time happy to see you again. He said you had the same eyes just as he remembered'.

Caitlin felt a lump in her throat as she tried to picture Kane as a sad old man. It was all too much for her, the tears she had been unable to cry now burst forth and streamed down her face. Mel tried to comfort her, *poor child how it grieved her to see her like this.* She wished there was something she could say, but words escaped her. However, she did have something up her sleeve and it was about to materialise. Before either of them could say another word the door bell rang.

'Ah' said Mel, 'I think I know who that will be, wait here dear child' she said getting up and shuffling to the door. Caitlin hurriedly dried her tears with her hand, she didn't want whoever it was to see her like that.

A short while later, Mel returned with the caller and when he came into the room, Caitlin nearly jumped out of her skin in surprise.

'Kane!' she shrieked and leaped to her feet, her heart pounding in her chest. She couldn't believe her own eyes, for there in front of her was Kane, or at least that was what she thought, since he looked exactly like him.

He smiled at her and said, 'pleased to meet you Caitlin, but my name's Jake not Kane'.

'Caitlin' said GG, 'Jake is Kane's Great Grandson'.

CHAPTER EIGHTEEN

Henry Pinkerton had long had a dream, a dream that he would be able to build a time machine and go back in time to the day his father died. Then he would do everything humanly possible to save him. However, this was never going to be possible, since although he had managed to construct his time machine, he was only able to go forward and back to the point at which the time machine had first been turned on and the vortex created. A practicality he was unable to resolve. Thus he was unable to realise his dream. However, somebody else was hopeful that he might be able to. That someone was Matt Jacobs. Matt was hoping that he could stop off in the year 2089, 21st July 2089 to be precise, the day his parents disappeared. He discussed it with the Professor, hoping that he would be able to oblige. The Professor listened to Matt and his heart went out to him. This was a man who suffered the same pain as himself, only worse, he had lost both of his parents. The difference was that it would be possible for Matt to return to the point at which his parents had disappeared, however, there was a moral dilemma to be considered. Should he allow him to do it? Was it right to risk changing time and the chaos that might ensue? They had already witnessed what evil minds could do when presented with such an opportunity. Matt, of course, was not evil and only had the best of intentions, however, there was still a lot at stake.

'You have to give me this chance' Matt implored him,

'I need to know what happened to them and if at all possible, save them'.

The Professor looked at the anguished face of a man tormented with years of not knowing what had become of his loved ones.

'Matt, I sympathise, but your actions could cause a rift in time, it's doubtful that you could even save them. There is a train of thought that time cannot be changed, what has happened has happened and even if we try, some power greater than us will render us unable to'.

Matt listened to what he was being told, but couldn't agree.

'There is also a train of thought that there is more than one possible future, that certain events can change the paths which are taken and who is to say that the present future cannot be changed?'

'I hear what you are saying Matt, but if I do decide to let you take the risk, you must promise that you will not deviate, that you will return as soon as you have either accomplished or failed in your mission, so that I can send you back to your own time and close the vortex forever'.

'You have my word Professor', Matt assured him.

The Professor was silent for a moment, deep in thought. Could he turn his back on his principles and let this young man achieve what he never could, or must he be cruel to be kind? Who would want to be him at that moment in time! After some considerable contemplation, the Professor had reached a decision.

'Okay Matt, I'll give you this one chance, but I warn you, things may not turn out as you would like them to, in fact, you may make matters worse'.

'I understand the risk, but it is one I am willing to take, thank you for your concern' Matt replied.

The Present Future

'Very well' said the Professor, *he hoped he wouldn't live to regret his decision.*

So Matt stepped into the vortex and as it swept him away from the year two thousand and eleven he felt slightly nauseous. He wasn't sure whether this was down to the side effects of time travel, or the anxiety of what he was about to face. When he emerged from the spiral of light, seventy eight years in the future, he had arrived in his past, on the very day that had haunted him ever since he was eight.

Luckily he found the Professor's laboratory deserted, as he was momentarily disorientated and a bit dizzy. The atmosphere in the laboratory was very eerie and he was glad to step out into the sunlight, even though the summer heat was intense and he had to shield his eyes from the bright midday sun. He was going to have to get himself motivated if he was going to make it to Exmouth marina on time. As to what he was going to do when he got there, he had no idea. If his recollection of that day was right, his mother dropped him off at his grandad's house at around ten past twelve, then went to pick up his dad before heading off for the marina. He remembered that day in great detail, right down to the pizza he had for lunch and how excited he felt about the prospect of going kayaking the next day. He remembered the last time he saw his mother's face smiling at him. He felt anxious about seeing her again, would she look the same to him now that he was nearer in age to her? Even though he knew that he would not be able to tell her who he was, or give her a big hug, it would be enough just to see her. The same could be said for his father. First he had to get to the marina and his best bet was to get the high speed sky train which ran continuously along the coastline from Seaton to Exmouth. He could catch it from Sidmouth, but he needed to hurry since he would need to be at Exmouth before one o'clock when his parents were due to meet the Mardell's by their motor launch at the marina.

He made his way down the cliff path to the town of Sidmouth below and was pleased to see that the sky train was waiting at the platform. He was also pleased to see the digital calendar on the platform which confirmed the date as being 21 July 2089, the Professor hadn't got his calibrations wrong! He just managed to jump on board the sky train before it departed at 12.30 pm. The journey to Exmouth would take ten minutes, just giving him enough time to sort himself out at the other end. His thoughts were interrupted by the train conductor saying 'tickets please'.

He felt bad about making the conductor believe the blank piece of card he held up to him was a ticket, but needs must, and it was for a worthy cause after all! Luckily for him the sky train employed human conductors rather than robots, otherwise he would have been stuck! He had no intention of using his abilities to steal or commit any other form of crime, but since his credits would not be valid in that time, he had no choice. He made a mental note to compensate the sky train service in some way in the future.

The train was crowded with tourists and locals alike, making the most of the nice weather. Matt scanned their faces to see if he recognised anybody, but nobody was familiar. It was quite surreal being there again, he thought about his younger self tucking into pizza and coke, totally oblivious to what was coming. As the train sped along parallel to the sea Matt looked out of the Perspex carriage, everything seemed so tranquil, he couldn't imagine how things could change so dramatically so as to swallow up the motor launch. In no time at all they were approaching Exmouth and Matt began to feel apprehensive. He was about to be given the answer to a question which had haunted him for years, namely what happened to his parents on that day. However, the even bigger question was, would he be able to prevent it from happening and if so, what was the damage likely to be? Would he go back to the future and find everything had changed? He shuddered at the thought, yet still he had to try, for the sake of that young lad eagerly awaiting their return.

On arriving at Exmouth Matt got off the train and headed over to the marina, he knew exactly where Jim Mardell's boat was moored. He walked past the pretty three storey houses, all painted in delicate pastels and along the wooden walkways until he came to the pontoon where he could see, much to his relief, that the motor launch was still moored up. He could hear voices coming from the cabin and recognised them as being Jim and Corrine Mardell. His parents were due to arrive any minute, so he would have to be quick. He needed to hire a boat in which to follow them.

Another vivid memory he had from his childhood was that of an old seafarer called Jock. Jock owned a small motor boat which he used to hire out to pay for his much beloved Jack Daniels. He gambled on the chance that both Jock and his boat would be there. It was certainly rare for Jock not to be, but there was a chance that somebody would already have taken the boat, especially on a day like that! He strolled along to where Jock could always be found and saw the familiar tanned, tattooed body sitting on a deck chair. He was also pleased to see the Mary Rose, Jock's prized boat, moored up. As he approached he could smell the distinctive aroma of Jack Daniels and guessed that Jock was probably well on the way to getting oiled. He was just at the point of saying something when he noticed that Jock was asleep, a glass of amber coloured liquid at his side. This gave him the opportunity he needed. Quietly and stealthily he snuck past Jock, watching him as he went to make sure he didn't wake up. Then with the nimbleness of a cat, he crept onto the Mary Rose, and was pleased to see that the key was in the ignition. Jock continued to sleep while Matt gently turned the key to the start position and flicked the master switch on. There was a high pitched beep. Matt pressed the ignition button and hoped for the best. The engine roared to life and so did Jock. On seeing that somebody was about to steal his precious boat he jumped out of the deck chair. He was about to yell, but for some reason he appeared to have lost his voice, his vocal chords would not work. *'Damn that Jack Daniels'* he thought to himself. No matter, he would stop this sucker before he got anywhere. He went to throw himself full pelt onto the Mary Rose but found that it wasn't only his voice that he had lost, but he also appeared to have lost the use of his legs as well since, try as he might, they just wouldn't move. It was like one of those dreams where you were being pursued by a giant beast but couldn't run way. That had to be it, he was dreaming, this wasn't really happening! He tried to pinch himself to prove the point, but was frozen rigid, unable to move any of his limbs. There was his answer, he was stuck in a horrible dream and soon he would wake up to find his beloved Mary Rose still resting silently in her moorings! He breathed a sigh of relief, luckily he was still able to do that!

Matt untied the Mary Rose from her moorings, then

gently steered her out of the marina to the open sea, where he waited for Jim's launch to follow.

CHAPTER NINETEEN

Vicki Jacobs was looking forward to cooling off by the coast, the heat was beginning to get to her. She just had to drop a reluctant Matt off at his grandad's, following which she would return home briefly to pick Nick her husband up, then they were to join the Mardells at Exmouth marina.

'Mum I want to come too' said Matt, deeply disappointed that he was missing out on a chance to get out on the water.

'Yes I know sweetheart, but this is just for grown ups, you'd get very bored', Vicki tried to placate him. 'I promise you we'll go kayaking at Exmouth tomorrow, how does that sound?'

'Cool, can we go to Tom's Diner afterwards?' asked Matt

'Of course, if you behave yourself' replied Vicki

'I will, thanks mum' Matt perked up a bit.

Vicki smiled, sometimes she forgot he was only eight, he seemed so grown up for his age. She had been full of concern when he had gone to see the Neurologist after the dizzy fits, she was afraid he may have some abnormality, but they had been unable to find anything wrong. His grandad seemed to think it was some genetic thing that he had inherited and there was nothing to worry about. Still she did worry about her only child and hoped that whatever it was he would grow out of it. She pulled up outside the Old Forge where Matt's grandad was sitting in the front garden enjoying the sun. On seeing them

The Present Future

arrive, he leapt up with the energy of a man half his age and bounded over to greet them.

'Hey big guy, fancy some pizza?' he said to his grandson fondly.

'Yeah' shouted Matt running up to give his grandad a big hug.

'Can I play with the Beetle Bots?' he asked full of expectation.

'Sure you can, but what's the magic word?' his grandad asked.

'Please' replied Matt.

'Off you go then' his grandad gestured for him to go into the house.

'Hey, aren't you forgetting something?' Vicki shouted after him. Matt turned round and shouted 'bye mum' before disappearing into the kitchen.

'Take care of him Bill' Vicki said to his grandad.

'You know I will' he replied winking at her, 'now you go off and have a good time, I'll see you later'.

'See you later' Vicki said before heading back to the car. In no time at all she arrived back home where Nick was waiting for her. Dressed in cream linen trousers and a mint polo shirt he looked every bit as handsome as the day she first set eyes on him. His thick dark hair blended perfectly with his tanned, sculpted face and those blue eyes, they were to die for!

'Are you ready for the off?' he asked, before planting a warm kiss on her lips making her heart skip a beat.

'Sure, I can't wait to get some of that sea air' she smiled back at him.

He watched as she slipped into the driver's seat, he couldn't help but admire her lean legs. She was wearing navy blue shorts and a white strappy top, which showed off her lovely figure. Her tawny brown hair was tied up in a knot, but several strands had managed to escape, giving her face the cheeky look of a teenager.

'Just as beautiful as the day we met' he said quietly to himself.

'What was that?' asked Vicki

'Nothing sweetheart, I guess we had better be going as time is getting on' he replied.

So on that note, they set off for the marina, totally oblivious to what was about to happen.

They arrived just before one o'clock. The motor launch was gleaming in the sunlight. Nick Jacobs preferred his boats to travel under sail, but he wasn't averse to a bit of lazing about on his friend Jim's motor launch every now and then. Today would have been a dead loss for sailing in any event since there was little wind. Jim and his wife Corrine were already on board when Nick and Vicki arrived. The small fridge was stocked up with beer and wine ready for the trip.

'Come aboard' said Jim, beckoning to them. He held out a hand for Vicki as she stepped off the pontoon onto the deck. He caught a whiff of her sun tan lotion as she nudged past him, it smelt as lovely as she looked. He had always had a soft spot for Vicki. She and Corrine had been friends at Uni where they first met and he had secretly hoped that Vicki would fall for him, but sadly she preferred Nick, the dashing marine instead. Such was life!

'You're looking lovely as ever' he said to Vicki, giving her the benefit of his pristine white teeth.

'Thanks Jim' she smiled, trying not to cringe, she had always found him a bit creepy. She was looking forward to spending some time on the water, especially as it was a scorcher of a day.

'Hi Vicky, how's things?' asked Corrine, peering at her from under a large straw sunhat. Being a redhead she was prone to freckles, which were entirely acceptable when one was a teenager, but now they just looked like age spots, so she was determined to keep them at bay!

'Hectic as always' replied Vicki, 'how about you?'

'Much the same' replied Corrine, 'so now we get to chill out and have some fun for a change, come take a pew' she patted the soft leather seat next to her. Vicki sat down gratefully.

'A glass of the usual?' Corrine asked.

'Oh, yes please' replied Vicki, her friend knew her only too well! Corrine reached into the fridge where there were some wine glasses chilling along side the drinks (it always made wine crisper somehow when poured into chilled glasses). She filled one of the glasses before handing it to an appreciative Vicki.

'Lovely, just what the doctor ordered' said Vicki taking a sip of the nectar.

'What about us?' said Jim, 'a man could die of thirst here!'.

'Okay, a little patience please' tutted Corrine, 'you'll have to have a soft drink as you're driving, what about you Nick?'.

'A beer for me' he replied, 'tough luck Jim'.

'No worries, I'll have a couple of beers on dry land later' replied Jim, before launching himself into the helm. He looked the part, wearing black and white stripy shorts, a T-shirt with skull and cross bones emblazoned on the front and a cap with a broad rim. Being slightly stocky and a few inches shorter than Nick, he reminded Vicki of a character out of one of Matt's favourite TV shows.

'Right crew, are we ready?' he addressed them all.

'Aye, aye Captain' replied Nick, causing Vicki and Corrine to giggle like school girls.

So they set off towards Ladrum, leaving the small marina behind them, none of them anticipating the events that were to follow on that calm afternoon. They didn't notice the mysterious man watching them from a small boat.

Matt followed the sleek blue and white motor launch as it left the marina. As he got nearer to it he could just about make out the silhouettes of four people. He had found some binoculars on board the Mary Rose and now lifted them to his eyes to get a closer look. Suddenly his mother's face was there right in front of him, she looked so young and beautiful. Seeing her there, looking so happy and carefree brought back all the pain of losing her. She was laughing at something the man standing next to her was saying. Matt focused the binoculars on the man and saw the familiar face of his father. He had never realised before just how much he resembled him, he had the same blue eyes and thick brown curly hair. He wanted to stay in that moment forever, but he knew that he couldn't, something awful was due to happen to those people very soon and he would need to act fast if he was going to stop it. He put the binoculars down and steered the Mary Rose in the same direction, not wanting to lose sight of them. He had no idea of what was to come.

The launch continued on its voyage and Vicki relished the cool breeze created by its slipstream. She marvelled at how beautiful the sea looked, sparkling with sunlight. There were a few other boats around and an abundance of kayaks, all making the most of the wonderful conditions. She thought about her son and how he would have loved to have been out there in one of those kayaks, never mind, she thought, tomorrow he would get his chance. She glanced at her husband, his tanned skin made the whites of his eyes look even whiter. She thought herself to be so lucky with her lot, she wouldn't change a thing. She could hear Jim chuckling away on the radio to somebody. Everything seemed to be perfect, then suddenly it all changed.

For some strange reason, the launch started to rock about as if encountering rough seas and Vicki found herself stumbling forward. Nick caught hold of her arm and helped her to sit down. He couldn't understand what was happening, and neither could Jim. He had stopped talking to whoever was on the other end of the radio as he tried frantically to maintain control of the launch. Nick managed to pull himself forward to where Jim was standing to see what he could do to help.

'I can't understand it' yelled Jim, 'the instruments have gone haywire'.

Nick looked at the compass and saw that it was spinning around madly, yet the boat was maintaining a straight course. He looked out to sea expecting to see an approaching squall, but the sky was clear blue and cloudless as before. It made no sense, where was this turbulence coming from?

'What the hell….look at that!' Jim pointed at something, the like of which he had never seen before. Nick looked to where he was pointing, he couldn't believe what he was seeing either, for there in the distance appeared to be what looked like a giant vortex of swirling light and they were heading right for it.

'Quickly turn this thing around' urged Nick.

Jim struggled with the wheel, but the elements seemed to be conspiring against him.

'I can't control her' he said in desperation.

They both stood watching helplessly as the giant vortex seemed to pull them ever closer.

Matt also watched from the Mary Rose, he was only a short distance away now, but he might as well have been on another planet. He felt sick and horrified by what he was witnessing, the vortex must have rippled when he opened it, just as it did when the Professor stepped out of it on the day the Super Vulcan made her maiden voyage. Now he understood what the Professor had meant when he talked about the dangers of trying to change time. Matt tried desperately to reach the motor launch, but the large waves were slowing the Mary Rose down. He watched as the events of the day unfolded in front of his eyes, the life long mystery was about to be solved in a way he could never have dreamt possible.

'Oh my god it was all my fault!' he gasped, at the realisation of what he had done, but it was no use. Within seconds Matt saw the motor launch, containing two of the people he loved most in the world, being sucked into the giant vortex, then in an instant as quickly as it had appeared, the vortex disappeared leaving the seas calm once again and Matt Jacobs, man and boy all alone.

THE END

Lightning Source UK Ltd.
Milton Keynes UK
19 December 2010

164632UK00001B/1/P